MW01043545

Flash in the *Pantheon*

Flash Fiction

123 Tales

Rhys Hughes

Gloomy Seahorse Press

Gloomy Seahorse Press
http://gloomyseahorsepress.blogspot.com

Table of Contents:

This melange
of very short stories
is dedicated to

Amira Ana Smyth

Author's Foreword

None of the following tales are longer than 999 words; most are much shorter. I suspect that an ideal flash fiction is always less than 500 words. Not long ago, works of this nature were known by the fairly clumsy name of 'short shorts' and king of the form was Fredric Brown. Saturated with puns and silly language twists, Brown's texts somehow manage to avoid being mere jokes. They are authentic tales; but the cliché that every story needs a beginning, middle and end *on the page* isn't true. It can be enough for a flash fiction author to provide one of the three, leaving the other two to enjoy a late existence in the reader's head.

There are many special categories of flash fiction and most are rather recent developments: the 'mini-saga', a complete tale in 50 words, not one more or less, dates back to the early 1980s and is the brainchild of Brian Aldiss; the more suggestive '69er' allows a microfiction writer to loll in the luxury of an extra nineteen words; and the 'drabble' (100 words long) is even more generous in this regard.

Some heavyweight authors indeed have been experts at flash fiction. I ought to mention the names of Franz Kafka, Jorge Luis Borges, Jean Cocteau and Italo Calvino; I will also point out that Russia often produces specialists in the art. Writers such as Mikhail Zoshchenko, Leonid Dobychin, Varlam Shalamov and the dark absurdist Daniil Kharms suggest there must be something in the vodka; or perhaps simply living under Stalin's regime persuaded one to write short and pithy to accurately reflect anticipated lifespans.

My favourite microfiction of all is a tale by John Barth that appears in his excellent collection *Lost in the Funhouse*. A pair of scissors and pot of glue are required to appreciate it, for the story consists of a strip of paper that must be twisted into a Möbius strip. Before the twist is made, the story is no more than ten words long; afterwards it becomes infinite. That's a very Borgesian trick; and Barth, an admirer of Borges, holds the distinction of writing the only never-ending story that is also a microfiction. But I was too timid to disfigure my own copy of Barth's book in the required manner.

The flash fictions in the following volume span almost my entire career as a writer. The earliest dates from 1991 and was my first published story; the most recent is from December 2013. I chose exactly one hundred and twenty three because I like that number, no more significant reason. Just to be a bit awkward, the three tales that begin with 'Postmodern Picnic' can be regarded as one story called 'Tribulation Trio', and the final twenty-one tales can also be regarded as a single multi-part fiction entitled 'The Floppiness of Mucky Puppet', if you wish to do so. If you don't, that's fine too. It doesn't really matter.

Goblin Sunrise

Anna shook her husband awake. Gareth blinked dreams from damp lashes. He struggled through the syrup of hypnopompic sleep. His yawn was as pink and large as the morning.

Anna kept shaking him. "Eh?" he gasped. His hands clenched the pillow and wrestled it over the edge of the bed. The reflexes of a tree, Anna thought derisively. His eyes snapped open.

"What is it? What's wrong?"

Anna lost no time. "There's a little man outside the window. He's wearing a floppy hat and curly slippers. He's laughing his head off. He's very ugly indeed. He has a dirty beard and a warty face. Also, he has got horns."

"Ah yes, that must be the goblin I ordered."

"The what?" Anna cast a doubtful look through the frosty glass. She frowned. "Did you say *goblin?*"

"Didn't I tell you? I ordered one yesterday to do some work for us. Very hard workers apparently, very efficient, very neat. Good overall value." Gareth yawned again.

"Where did you order it from?"

"Little People Inc. A company based in Cork, Eire. They provide goblins, gnomes, dwarves, elves and leprechauns for customers. Goblins are the cheapest of the lot. Not very bright, you see, but good workers all the same. Beautiful," he added.

Anna pouted. "I see." She lay back down on the bed. Gareth closed his eyes. Anna frowned once more. Gareth snored. After a couple of minutes, she turned on her side, propped herself up on one elbow and studied his face with its gaping, drooling mouth.

"What now?" He was somehow aware of her

intense gaze.

"Let me get this straight. You ordered a goblin to do some work for us? What sort of work?"

"Oh, in the garden." He was dismissive.

There was another long pause. "I see," she said again. She scratched her nose. She introduced the toes of her left foot to the toes of her right. "Then why is he floating in the air? And why is he cutting at the clouds with a pair of clippers?"

"What?" Gareth woke with a start, jumped out of bed and squinted in the early light. The sun was big and red on the horizon. And there, far away, silhouetted by the dawn, a goblin was carefully trimming the rosy cumulus tufts.

Gareth opened the window, looked down at his overgrown garden, shook his fists at the sky and cried, "The lawn, you fool! The *lawn!*"

Sexing the Confection

The baker turned his crusty eyes upon my purchase. "Chocolate éclairs. What use are they in sex?"

"I beg your pardon?" I had no desire to linger. My girl awaited me in my garret. We have an original kink, which I shall keep secret for another nine paragraphs.

"Don't be coy. I know your type. I've worked here for a decade. You don't copulate like I do. I've watched."

I gulped. "You have?"

The baker bent closer. His whisper was a hiss of deflating pastry. I parted the miasma of his yeasty breath and saw his baguette-like chin looming over the counter.

"I followed one chap home. Peered through his window. Saw him with his macaroon. Unnatural it was. Disgusting!"

Clutching my bag, I crept towards the door. The baker broke down in a flood of tears. "My wife refuses to do it with me. We can never have cakes of our own!"

Trembling, I managed to open the door without sounding the bell. I took to my heels and reached my attic. Celia was already there, having returned from her own bakery.

We placed our prizes on the table. I teased her doughnut onto one end of the varnished surface. She agitated my bag until the éclairs spurted forth onto the other.

We sat back exhausted. Over the following week, the éclairs would struggle towards their destination. Most would fall by the wayside, but we hoped at least one would make it.

We are trying to breed gateaux.

The Spanish Cyclops

There was a lens grinder who had fallen on hard times and who decided to revive his fortunes by exceeding the limits of his profession. Accordingly, he saved his remaining materials and set to work on the grandest project he could imagine.

The citizens of Valencia were perturbed at the noises that emanated from his workshop during the days and nights of a whole week.

At last he threw open his doors and rolled out

into the town square the largest monocle in the world. It glittered below the green lamps that hung from the taverns and theatres. And soon a crowd gathered.

"What is the purpose of this object?" they wondered.

They walked around it, touching it lightly. It was too big to fit a king or bishop or even the statue of El Cid that loomed on the battlements of the palace. No eye in history might wear it comfortably in a squint. It was clear the lens grinder had lost his sanity.

The soldiers came to lock him up in a madhouse, but he stalled them with an explanation. They rattled their pikes uneasily.

He said, "The entity for whom this monocle was made will seek it out when he learns of its existence, and he will pay me handsomely, because he has waited to see properly again for centuries."

There was much speculation as to the nature of this customer. People mounted the city walls to look out for him, but they saw nothing when they gazed inland. Once they called out that he was coming, yet it was only an elephant being led to a circus in Barcelona. Excitement and fear surged together.

While they watched, a ship from Cathay sailed into the bay and the citizens turned their attention out to sea. Even from this distance, the cargo of spices could be smelled. But as the vessel entered the harbour, a gigantic whirlpool opened up and sucked it down. The crew and all the pepper were destroyed.

A cry of horror filled the streets and bells were rung in more than a hundred churches. Then someone remembered the great circular eyepiece and called out for help in rolling it down to the quayside. Within a minute, a crowd of volunteers was pushing at the rim of the monocle, bouncing it over the cobbles like a burning wheel.

The lens grinder followed helplessly, tearing at his hair as his marvellous creation gathered speed. Soon it slipped out of the grasp of the thousand hands and trundled along a jetty and over the edge.

There was no splash. The monocle landed in the eye of the whirlpool, fitting it perfectly. Men and women rushed onto the jetty and peered over the side, gasping in wonder at what they beheld.

The ocean was no longer blind. As the whirlpool moved across the bay, it revealed the gardens of the deep. Through the sparkling lens it was possible to discern the seabed in astonishing clarity. And now all the wrecks of ages past were focussed on the surface, the gold and gems and casks of wine.

A few citizens jumped into boats and chased the roving eye to the horizon and beyond. They made maps as they did so, noting the position of each trove, planning for a future time when the treasures might be hauled up and distributed equally among the population, or perhaps they were just enjoying the spectacle.

There was general rejoicing, but the lens grinder went home in some trepidation and awaited a very big knock on his door.

Gone With the Wind in the Willows

The Confederate Army was shelling Toad Hall. Down in the bunker, Toad and Ratty were cowering under a table, drinking bourbon. Plaster fell from the ceiling and filled the room with fine dust. "Where the hell is

General Badger?" Toad wailed.

Just at that moment, Mole erupted from the floor, a message clamped between his jaws. Toad snatched the communiqué and devoured the spidery words with his rheumy eyes. "Badger's forces have been eliminated on the outskirts of Atlanta."

"Oh my, we're doomed!" avowed Ratty.

Toad drained his glass of bourbon and puffed on a cigar. "Time for the cyanide and petrol, boys."

Screams of terror reached them from outside. It seemed the entire Confederate Army was on the run. The door to the bunker flew open and a svelte figure stood framed by licking flames.

"I came as quickly as I could," it said.

"Who the hell are you?" Toad cried.

"Bambi," it replied. It trotted into the room. "I know I'm not in your story, but I couldn't sit and watch you be annihilated. I've brought the Hollywood Infantry with me."

"I'll be darned, a goddamn postmodernist!"

"Not quite. What's that you're drinking? Bourbon? May I have some? I've got a tankard with me. Will you fill it up?"

"You are joking. This is vintage stuff."

"I'll settle for just a wine glass of the liquor in that case."

"No way. This is expensive 108 proof Wild Turkey Rare Breed with a kick like an electrocuted whore."

"Well how about filling a whisky glass? I only want a taste."

Toad climbed from under the table and sneered. "Frankly, my deer, I don't give a dram."

14

The Backwards Aladdin

The lamp was as Persian as a carpet made from a fluffy cat.

Niddala rubbed it with her sleeve and told the emerging figure that she didn't want to spend all her wishes at once. Was interest available on those she saved for later?

The blue creature shook its head. "The old stories got it wrong. I'm only compelled to give you one wish and you have to use it right now."

"In that case, I wish for more wishes!"

"That's not permitted."

"What if I wish for you to fall in love with me? That way you'll always be happy to do anything I ask."

"That's also against the rules."

Niddala protested but the creature had no sympathy and merely added, "You're running out of time."

So she said, "I wish I was a genie."

"Very clever!" hissed the apparition in dismay but it waved its hands and there was a blinding flash. After the smoke cleared, Niddala found herself wearing a turban.

"Now I can do what I like."

"No you can't!" roared the bald being. "That's not how genies work. You have to *grant* wishes to others!"

Immediately it pounced on her and rubbed her stomach furiously. "I wish I was human!"

Niddala's arms seemed to acquire a life of their own, describing strange shapes in the air. Another flash and the creature had shrunk to a normal size. He was still bald but now he was the colour of human skin. His laughter was full of desperate relief.

"Free at last! I'm a man!"

"Wait a moment," said Niddala. "Are you sure a genie is allowed to rub another genie? That doesn't seem right somehow. I wouldn't trust the result of such a wish. The effect might wear off."

"I hadn't thought of that. But I'm a man now and you're a genie and I haven't had my wish *as a man* yet, so I'm going to reconfirm my decision."

He leaned forward with raised hands, rubbed her stomach again and called, "I wish I was human!"

But nothing happened. Niddala sighed.

"You can't wish to be something you already are. That's not a wish but a grammatical error. A wish implies a yearning for a lack. You can't lack a quality which you have."

"I hate the pitfalls of logic!" came the exasperated reply. "Let me think of a different wording. I have it! I wish *not* to be a genie."

This time arms were waved. Smoke.

Niddala blinked at the object that existed before her. It seemed to consist of everything at once, or parts of everything, or parts of an unimaginable number of other parts. The colours were scintillating. Then she understood what had happened.

"You fool! You've accidentally wished to be *everything* that isn't a genie! Not being a genie is a quality that *all* things *except* genies possess. You've become a universal soup!"

The reply was trillionfold. "Yes, and I don't feel well."

Niddala arched an eyebrow. "I'm not surprised." Then an idea came to her. She reached into the unbelievable swirl and felt around for a moment before rubbing the smooth and large something she finally found. "I wish to be Niddala!"

Instantly she was back to her former self.

Before she departed she explained, "If you are everything other than a genie, then you must also be whatever it is that genies rub to get wishes from. I think I'll go shopping now."

She looked back over her shoulder. "You don't happen to have a place that sells carpets in there, do you?"

The Man who Gargled with Gargoyle Juice

"It's good for your throat."

"I'm not sure. I don't like the sound of it. I bet the taste is awful. Will it be very slimy?

"Not slimy. Not slimy at all."

"The goblin was slimy."

"Surely it was. That's the only kind we get round here, the slimy ones. If you were to go as far north as Kilkenny you might be able to procure a powdery goblin or maybe even a peppery one, but down here in Cork the goblins spend a lot of time above ground in the rain and the water gets inside them."

"Don't they wear capes and boots?"

"Certainly they do, but the capes and boots on sale in Cork are the porous kind, full of little holes."

"Won't you try me with a leprechaun or fairy first?"

"That would be a waste of your money. The fluid inside a leprechaun is less potent than goblin juice and you've already drunk a goblin to no avail.

As for fairies they are out of season and you'd have to cross the equator into the southern hemisphere to get one at this time of year. That would be very expensive."

"How about a banshee?"

"This is a shop, not a story. Banshees don't really exist. Neither do trolls, hippogriffs or golems."

"Maybe some antibiotics would do the trick?"

"I don't think so. You must have a very severe throat infection if a goblin didn't cure it. The kind of medicine you get from a doctor won't stand a chance. You've come to the right place now and I'm sure gargoyle juice is the best remedy."

"Where do you get your ingredients from?"

"A local company, Little People Inc. They send agents out with nets to explore grottoes, climb churches, sleep under toadstools and do whatever else is necessary to replenish stock."

"Is there only one method of extracting the juice?"

"Absolutely not. Goblins are simply popped into the liquidiser but pixies are pressed by hand through a sieve. As for gnomes they have to be hung by their feet and tickled until all the fluid has dripped into a bucket. Gargoyles are different again."

"Repeat that in a more typically Irish manner, will you?"

"The divil I will! Be off with your strange requests! Do you want to get rid of your sore throat or not?"

"Yes I do. I'll try a gargoyle if you really think it will help. Do they take long to prepare? How much are they?"

"It won't burn a hole in your pocket. Trust me. Wait here and I'll have the drink ready for you in a few minutes. You won't regret this, I assure you."

"What's that odd wheezing sound?"

"That's just me working the bellows in the back room. Just stay there in the front of the shop and I'll rejoin you soon enough. Why not tell me about yourself while you are waiting?"

"I don't know where to begin."

"Birth is the standard opening to a human life. Maybe your mother was a woman with big hands? Maybe she walked on stilts and kissed the tops of chimneys? Was she a duck in a former existence? Perhaps her forearm resembled the coast of Norway? Did she meet your father on a gangplank? Did she sleep in an awkwardly varnished bed?"

"I have simply no idea."

"No matter. I was only making small talk. The gargoyle juice is ready now. I'll bring it out to you. Be sure to drink it all down in one gulp for maximum effect. Here it is."

"A stone cup with insulated handles?"

"Yes indeed. Be careful how you hold it. That's right, pour it down your throat, every last drop. Sure it glows like lava. That's because it *is* lava, a gargoyle taken from a Cork church melted down in my furnace. So what do you think? Do you like it?"

"Urgh! Nunnghrrrgh!"

"That was clumsy of you, dropping the cup like that! Of course it burns terribly. What did you expect? A gargoyle is a small sculpture, a stone figure, not a living creature like a goblin. The juice of a gargoyle is several thousand degrees centigrade, otherwise it turns solid again. But it's guaranteed to stop a sore throat."

19

"Aaaarghgh! Eerughfffghghghgh!"

"I'll have to guess what that means. Are you trying to say that this wasn't quite what you expected? Maybe not. But you can't have a sore throat when you have no throat. Gargoyle juice never fails. I've treated hundreds of patients this way and not one ever voiced a complaint afterwards!"

The Iron Age

The men sprawled on the sand in the sun. The beach was vast, a curve of gold that bracketed an emerald sea; and although the sunlight was fierce, the shadows of the coconut palms were sharp: there was no heat haze, no shimmering mirages. It was a perfect coastline, an elegant fragment of a scene from a daydream turned into reality by some benign cosmic force, a segment of paradise, tropical, munificent.

Viewed from above, the men lay between the shadows of the trees like prisoners emerging from cages whose bars were spaced too far apart. And it *was* possible to gaze down on the men this way. Hang-gliders spiralled overhead, just a few of them, taking care never to block the sun, never to come between the blazing source of all life on the planet's surface and the men who worshipped it flat on their backs.

The men continued to absorb the rays into their taut skin. Slowly they ripened, acquired the sheen of ancient shields, and there was no danger of sunburn here, no risk of cancer, for this was an earlier era, a period before humankind had damaged the atmosphere, before industrial fumes, factory emissions, aerosol pollutants. The hang-gliders had wicker frames, wings stitched from leaves. Nature was in balance.

The pilots of the gliders were women, the mates of the men. While the men did what they had to do, basking in the sun and darkening their skin, the women played. They flew or surfed the waves or dived for treasure in the shallows near the reefs or climbed cliffs and sea stacks without ropes. Intrepid, fearless, curious: the females were the active ones. That was the rule of this culture, the way things had to be.

A tiny figure appeared at the far end of the beach and began shuffling through the sand towards the men. It was hunched and muffled in a cloak and it used a crooked stick as an aid to walking. The men did not notice the stranger until he was almost upon them. The women stopped playing and watched, standing in the surf or circling in the sky, as the ungainly figure finally paused and noisily cleared his throat.

One of the sunbathing men sat up, blinking at the new arrival. He saw an old face framed by the hood of the cloak, a long white beard and skin that was horribly pale. Unable to comprehend the character of the visitor, bemused by his peculiar garb, the man continued to blink, saying nothing and not even opening his mouth to gape. His companions also sat up and they all waited, slightly sleepy but uneasy.

The hooded figure cleared his throat again. "I have news. My task is to bring this news to every community on every beach in the world. Nothing lasts forever, that is the miserable truth."

"What do you mean?" cried the men together.

"My friends, it gives me no satisfaction to make this announcement. I am merely a messenger, nothing more."

"Very well. But what is your message?"

The hooded figure raised his stick and made a sweeping gesture with it that encompassed everything in existence.

"The Bronze Age is over. It's over, I tell you! Over!"

"The Bronze Age is over? But—"

"The Iron Age is here instead. It has arrived *now*!"

And the stick continued to spin and the tip of it seemed to be breaking the surface of a pond; but that pond was the sky, the sea, the sand, and it disrupted the image of the world as it was, replacing the old reality with a new one, so that when the pond settled the images had all changed. Walls rose up, as if flat areas of the beach had fused into squares, and part of the sky came down, encasing the men indoors.

They stood and shivered. Suddenly it was very cold.

Where had the tropical paradise gone?

There were tiny high windows set in the walls, but no sunlight beyond the grimy glass, only thick grey clouds.

The hooded figure had also changed: he was now a pile of clothes in a laundry basket in a corner. Ironing boards had been set up throughout the room and electric irons hissed like conspirators. Stepping over the cables that connected these spitting devices with the wall sockets, the men knew instinctively what to do. The bronze of their skin was already fading into the colour of rancid milk. They set to work.

The Bronze Age was over. It was the Iron Age at last.

The steam from the irons billowed.

The war against creases had finally begun.

Waiting for Breakfast

A boy sat on the beach with a toasting fork, holding it up to the sun. "You need to light a fire with driftwood," the sun told him, "because I'm not hot enough to toast that slice of bread."

"You will be when you turn into a Red Giant," answered the boy.

The sun considered this and said:

"Yes, I'll swell up and engulf the innermost planets and boil into steam the oceans of Earth, and any bread lying around will toast nicely, but that won't happen for billions of years!"

The boy laughed and shook his head.

"Don't you know that one day I'll have children and entrust this task to them, and that they too will have children and do likewise, and so on until the necessary time has elapsed?"

The sun was amazed. "That *is* a long wait for breakfast!"

The Dark Horse

"The problem finally has a solution," said Mr Angelo as Mr Dobbs entered the classroom. The children had gone home, the silence throughout the school seemed unnatural, almost oppressive on the ears.

"Really?" Mr Dobbs stumbled as he approached.

Mr Angelo nodded. "Yes, I think so, I honestly think so. Miss Gentle has offered to sort things out for us…"

"Miss Gentle?" Mr Dobbs snorted. "But she only joined the school a few weeks ago! What experience does she have in such matters?" And he indicated the classroom, the objects that filled it.

Mr Angelo chose his words with care. "Well, it seems… it seems she's a dark horse… That's the blunt truth."

"Are you sure about this?"

Mr Angelo nodded vigorously. "Almost certain. I casually mentioned the problem to her yesterday in the staff room and she immediately came out with a suggestion. It was a very good suggestion but I doubted her ability to implement it. Then she bared her teeth at me in a particular way and I suddenly took her very seriously."

"So Miss Gentle is a dark horse? Well, well!" Mr Dobbs stumbled again and felt an apple crush itself under his shoe; the tang of juicy pulp rose to his nostrils. "I just hope it works."

"Me too." Mr Angelo glanced at the clock on the wall. "She'll be here any minute now. I want you to be a witness."

Mr Dobbs made a gesture that encompassed the entire classroom. "It's like an orchard after a fierce storm…"

"I keep writing to the parents, but it doesn't do any good." Mr Angelo puffed out his cheeks. "Please don't give your child apples as presents for teacher, I tell them. They don't listen. Every day another thirty apples. Week after week. I'm overflowing with the damn things and there's almost no room to move and—"

He was interrupted by the clip-clop of hooves in the corridor beyond the door. There was a loud snort.

"Enter!" cried Mr Angelo and Miss Gentle trotted in.

She paused and gazed at the apples.

"Hundreds of them!" exclaimed Mr Angelo. "Do you think you can manage? Do you really?" He blinked.

Miss Gentle wasted no time. She began eating...

Mr Angelo turned to Mr Dobbs. "What did I tell you? She's a dark horse without question."

"But she has a—" Mr Dobbs was unable to finish the sentence.

They watched her munch her way through the selection of apples, the red, orange and green varieties, the sour and sweet kinds, crunching peel, stalk and pips between her long teeth with as much relish as the succulent flesh, making space in the classroom, tail swishing from side to side, ears twitching, her black mane hanging low.

"That's enough work for one day, Miss Gentle," said Mr Angelo eventually. "We don't want you to get indigestion. Come back at the same time tomorrow." He added for Mr Dobbs' benefit, "Shouldn't take more than a week to clear them away."

Miss Gentle trotted out of the room and clip-clopped back down the corridor. Mr Angelo beamed. "See?"

"What?" Mr Dobbs was pale and shaking.

"She really was a dark horse!"

"No, no, no!" spluttered Mr Dobbs, collapsing into the nearest chair, a child's chair, the knees of his long legs at the same level as his shoulders. "Didn't you notice? She had a horn growing out of her head! She's not a dark horse at all! What have you done to this school? It's against all the regulations. You've employed a — a unicorn!"

In Moonville

In Moonville when the sun goes down, the people go out to moonbathe in the streets, to drink moonshine and moon around. They love the moon in that town. I think it was Frabjal Troose who established the fashion for all things lunar. Or perhaps he just took advantage of an existing impulse.

(They tell me he was a wealthy man, and at first I doubted this, because I did not know who 'they' were, but after dwelling in Moonville for several months I began to realise that 'they' equally did not know who 'I' was. So then I felt some sort of balance had been achieved and I decided to believe them.)

His house still stands in the darkest shadows of that place, almost blotted out by other roofs, empty and forlorn. Even the strange servants have abandoned it, the giant clockwork puppets and musical monkeys. Once he held parties in that house for his neighbours and other moonlighting couples, but now it is a silent shell.

Moonville is full of roofs, mounted on pillars above each other at curious angles, and nobody is surprised at the number of things that get lost beneath them. They multiply at an astounding rate and the noise of building work rarely ceases during the day. But the people would have it no other way, for it is the roofs that bring the moon closer.

Even though they love only the moon, the people have not forgotten Frabjal Troose and sometimes they tell anecdotes about him. Most of these anecdotes are blatant lies and others are more subtle distortions of the truth, often misinterpretations of what actually happened. But few are malicious and some are even sympathetic.

For instance, they mention the time he was attacked by a *clock-a-lot*, a mechanical monster of his own devising. He was found unconscious among scattered cogs and springs and splinters of wood. His claim that he accidentally toppled a large timepiece on himself was generally disregarded.

I noticed how many of these anecdotes involved unusual machines. On another occasion, after trimming his fingernails with a small scissors, he invented a device that amplified and translated the speech of very small animals. The first time he switched it on, he distinctly heard a line of ants exclaim:

"Look what we have found: tusks! The tusks of unknown creatures!"

Then he watched the ants carry back the fingernail clippings as trophies, like big game hunters, perhaps to decorate the walls of their nest. When I hear such stories I grow impatient. I want to know about Moonville itself, about its domestic relationship with the moon. Absurd digressions only hinder my work.

"Not so!" they reprimand me. "All the books in

this town are full of digressions. In fact most of them are entirely and absurdly digressive, to the point where nobody can be sure what any of them are really about, even though they are about many things."

In Moonville the art of reading clearly lacks clarity. Only love for the moon is precise and unchanging. When the moon rises or sets in the other towns of the world it appears bigger, as big as it ever can be, but when it is high in the sky it seems smaller. Not so in Moonville. In Moonville it is always huge, bloated and serene and visibly bruised.

To keep the moon always on the horizon, the inhabitants of Moonville began adding extra roofs to their houses, balancing a succession of artificial horizons on each other, chasing the moon to its highest point. Now the town is a town of roofs, as overbalanced as a man wearing too many hats.

At first there was a danger of walling themselves in, building a shell from the inside that would blot out the moon and everything else. But Frabjal Troose proposed a solution, separating the roofs on very slender pillars, so the light of the moon was never obscured. It simply climbs from one horizon to another and the people redirect their gaze each time.

I believe a similar solution was arrived at in the town of Sunsetville, whose inhabitants love the sunset as much as the citizens of Moonville adore the moon. When the moon is on the horizon it seems much closer. But Frabjal Troose created disquiet by publicly declaring that closer was not close enough.

He was exiled from Moonville for his negative comments. Until a cheap method can be found for actually reaching the moon, the best option is to live in a town piled high with roofs. Frabjal Troose disagreed. He moved to a quiet spot far away, bought a small sea and paid for it to be entirely drained. He bathes dryly in it every day.

Or so they say. He was not missed. For every individual exiled from Moonville, a hundred new families arrive and settle. The town is expanding at an amazing rate. The same is apparently true for Sunsetville. One day the two towns will meet and mesh, and who can say for sure what will happen next?

Get a Room

I don't understand what the problem is with the rain and wind in Wales. The rain never falls vertically but insists on being blown sideways by the wind. The rain just won't ever appear on its own. Always it has to come together with the wind. Are they lovers or something? If they are, I wish they would *get a room* and leave me alone while I'm out and about!

Today I leave my house in my raincoat as usual, because there's no point taking an umbrella that is sure to be blown inside-out within a few seconds, but I don't feel buffeted by the wind and I don't feel any raindrops spattering me. I risk lowering my hood and then I see—

Blue sky and sun! In Wales! It's unheard of.

Whistling a tune, I skip merrily.

I pass a hotel near the train station and all the windows of the building are wide open with the exception of one in the highest corner. I look more carefully and I can see broken furniture being thrown

around inside that room and water cascading down
the pane on the inside.

"About time!" I mutter to myself as I hurry on.

The Planet of Perfect Happiness

The planet of perfect happiness is called Inclova and
it is important that visitors are aware how to explore it
safely. From space it appears exactly like a fictional
description of itself, a world of beautiful oceans and
delightful islands and continents covered in trees
heavy with delicious fruit, but when one actually
lands on it one soon learns that written accounts are
insufficient to convey the true allure of the place. It is
infinitely enticing. For many years visitors simply
leapt out of their spacecrafts onto the surface and then
they were lost. We are more careful now and take
suitable precautions.

A visitor who is unaware of the peculiar
hazards of perfect happiness will arrive at Inclova
eager to be greeted by the smiling people he has seen
strolling the forest glades or swimming the warm surf.
The moment he leaves his spacecraft and approaches
them it will seem to him that they have vanished. The
forests will be deserted, the surf empty, and worse
than this, he will vanish himself. In a rush of
confusion he will be aware only of intermittent
flashes around him, then a sense of reeling, of falling
into a runaway future, followed by oblivion, a natural
death from old age.

This planet is not a deliberate trap. It just so
happens that our moods dictate the velocity of time. A
painful or boring event slows time, whereas an

exciting or joyful event speeds it up. The happiness in Inclova is perfect. Therefore time reaches its maximum velocity. The inhabitants are barely aware they are alive before those lives are finished. To an outside observer, everything proceeds at a normal pace, the lives under scrutiny are full and measured. The moment this observer steps over the threshold of his spacecraft and becomes part of the planet, suffused with its perfect happiness, he loses his grip on his own existence.

The old methods of entering Inclova safely have been discredited. An assistant with a long pole would stand inside the open airlock of the spacecraft and jab the visitor at frequent intervals to keep him in pain and thus slow down his subjective sense of passing time. But if the visitor ventured beyond the pole's reach he was doomed. Cords tied around his neck and tightened from afar also failed. These cords became snagged on trees or were entangled around the legs of inhabitants visible from inside the spacecraft but invisible from the planet's surface, so rapidly did they live their lives, one blink from birth to death.

The only reliable technique is to stuff the visitor's many pockets with letters. Every ten paces he reaches for a letter and reads it. The first is from his father: he has been disinherited. The second is from his employer: he has no job to return to. The third is from his girlfriend: she no longer loves him. And so on. Whether these letters are true or not is irrelevant. The regular reinforcement of bad news will keep him miserable enough to explore Inclova without plummeting instantly into a vertical future. The more pockets he has, and the more to regret, the longer his possible stay on that blissful, deadly world.

There are other perfectly happy planets — once a planet laughed itself off its own axis — but they will not be discussed here.

NOTE: The planet of perfect happiness, Inclova, can be pronounced either as "In Clover" or "Ink Lover." Both are correct and appropriate in meaning. But the name is actually an anagram of the surname of Italo Calvino, author of *Invisible Cities*, the book that inspired the composition of this piece.

The Cloudhouse

I know a man who lives in the desert. He keeps a little cloud that waters his garden once a day. The cloud lives in a wooden box that is fixed to a very tall pole. In the evening, the cloud floats serenely out of its house and relieves itself. And then it floats serenely back in and sleeps the sleep of the clouds. Thus the man has a garden that overflows with fruits and all manner of good things. But as a hermit who also dwells in the desert, I am troubled by this man. I fear his actions will encourage other clouds. I do not want rain cooling the sores that cover my body or washing away the lice that infest my hair.

I decide to destroy this man by telling God all about him. I pick up the telephone and try to speak with God, but I can only ever get through to his secretary. God, she insists, is always away at business meetings. I explain the problem, but she can offer little useful advice. It seems that I will have to cut down the Cloudhouse myself, shake the cloud out of bed and stamp it to a puddle on the ground. Meanwhile, I can see the other clouds gathering on the borders of my desert. I shake my fists at them, I make rude gestures. My rage is turned against their fluffy aspirations. My misery is greater than ever before. I have never been happier.

Celia the Impaler

The story of a woman who has made love to six of the Seven Wonders of the World, causing them to collapse from exhaustion, and how she attempts to seduce the seventh and last, the Great Pyramid of Cheops, unaware that it cannot fall down, because a pyramid exists in the shape of a building which has already fallen down. Told from the viewpoint of the capstone.

Silence is a threnody for she who cries in no dark; not tears but words, or the spaces between words. I have her now in the thirst of noon, lapping the shores of her knees, back arched painfully aware and heavy with dust. She is rigid but not as stone, tormented but not by fresh desire; her lusts are as old as any morning in a life. And yet high above the cold vapours of her shallows, mouth exhaling webs of breath, scent spiralling from skin and hair, I also watch.

She climbs higher along my crumbling limbs. The shimmer coils her neck; reality has its way with her peripheral vision. We recall in her graceful motion some aspect of our own reaching upward. Block upon block, grains hissing in mouth, a smile not for myself nor yet for you. Teeth not quite straight, yet not crooked; lips snarled in a chapped curl, tongue anticipating, fingers seeking. From heavy bliss to the moment of release, one pant exchanged for another, in a different key.

Down below, you are innocent enough, entranced by vendors, colours, the wailing of a dozen new guides. You have chosen not to follow; your wife is always playing such pranks, slipping out of your reach to explore the inaccessible. You do not even bother to follow her reclining figure with your eyes. You light a cigarette and rejoice in the small throat burn, the tiny blink. Up there it is for real.

The chance is beyond you now: the sun like a pool of ice is the screen. I wait with patience infinite as she picks her way towards the resolution I can provide. Already I have your secrets, your failures, revealed to me in the tension of her muscles. All the rage in her disappointment, known to all but yourself. They laugh, those who smile at you in the evenings, clustered around an empty bottle of useless wine. You are the spring of their indulgent wit; they almost love you for it. Almost kiss you.

Tell me, callow friend, what would you do if you knew the truth? Would you scramble up after her, chin held high, calling her name in impotent rebuke? Probably not. Chest too tight, heart too small, even down here. You sit on a smooth cube of rock and swelter, because you never swelter in the dirt. Besides, it is too late now: she is nearly at the top, where I linger as her lover, and her arms are clawing towards me. You are lost.

Let me remind you of that time in Rhodes, in Ephesus, in Babylon and the rest. They are the wonders; but for her there is only one source of wonder. The ache between her legs and how it is gouged free. Those others were mere flirtations; conjectures, the foreplay of possible sites, all flaccid

34

from some earlier passion. Even then she asked you to come along, guessing that you would refuse. I am the consummation, the logical conclusion, the one remaining marvel.

Now she is up beside me, astride me, above me. I am a noble paramour and a deceitful one; I will take your wife's virginity for my own. Breathlessly, she hitches up her skirt and lowers herself onto my apex. The horns are yours, blistering youth, and you will never be able to justify your anger. The nuptial juice floods down my sides, slanting to the beds of sand all around, and her thighs glisten and undulate. Shall I reveal at last why I am the only one still standing, the seventh and best? No.

Love Keys

In a northern city or perhaps a southern one there was a footbridge made of metal that spanned a wide grey river in a low and not ungraceful arch. One end of this bridge was located near an art gallery and the other wasn't too far from a mighty cathedral with an impressive dome. It was extremely pleasant to cross this bridge in either direction and many people took advantage of it, sometimes just for the delight of making the crossing rather than because they really wanted to reach the far side of the water. It was a perfect place for a stroll, which is why strollers were attracted to it from every part of the city.

Over time this bridge acquired the reputation of being a romantic structure and lovers adopted it as their own, though it could be true that the lovers arrived first and the reputation later. Nobody really knows. At any rate, these lovers took with them little padlocks inscribed with their initials, often surrounded by hearts, and they secured the locks to the railings and cast the keys over the side. It was a tradition that spontaneously arose, as such customs often do, and the idea was to dramatically symbolise how the couple in question were locked together forever and that the only means of escape was lost.

The authorities didn't dare put a stop to this practice, despite the fact that the weight of so many locks on the footbridge was a cause for concern among the engineers who designed it, because for most citizens adding a lock was a wistful, charming, beautiful, funny, touching, sweet gesture, the very epitome of youthful optimism expressed in a simple act of commitment to another human being. Nor did the manufacturers of padlocks complain much. In fact the practice is what the bridge became most famous for, despite its excellent location and the tremendous views from various points along its length.

Eventually the locks accumulated to such an extent that no railing had one spare place for another to be added, so new lovers began securing their own locks to locks already in position. The bridge did sag a little but still no one came with a hacksaw to cut the locks off. And then one morning it was noticed that when a key was thrown into the river it no longer made a splash but a tinkling sound and that the mass of discarded keys was forming an island that had been rising out of the water for years and was now breaking the surface. But lovers still came to put padlocks on the span and jettison the keys.

And so this island grew to maturity and became established as an unofficial but important geographical feature of the city. A brand new custom arose for men and women who were no longer in love to swim or row out to the isle and search for the key that would open their own particular lock. It was nearly impossible to identify the right key by sight alone, so they would simply select a key at random and return to shore and cross the bridge and try it in their own lock, which rarely opened. Standing there, unable to open the symbol of their enjoinment to another person, they would be filled with frustration.

Instead of flipping the useless key over the side, vindictiveness or curiosity would get the better of them and they would systematically try it in every lock until one of them sprang open. To complete this malign act, they generally threw the open padlock over the railings and onto the isle of keys; and over a period of time the locks began to outnumber the keys, as if some bizarre geological process was at work. Couples would split up when they discovered their locks were gone, each blaming the other and venting their anger by visiting the island to take a key and spoil the relationship of some other pair.

Thus the locks vanished from the bridge one by one until none remained at all. But this is the truly odd thing: unbeknown to anyone, the bridge had already decayed away. Only the locks had remained intact and their complex interlinking had formed a substitute structure, a chain of love that spanned the water, so when they were removed the bridge ceased to exist. It was dismantled by the power and ingenuity of sadness until the river flowed just as it had done before the building of the footbridge, and the two halves of the city, once in love but no longer, were separated by the oily currents of circumstance.

The Wrexham Chainsaw Massacre

In the dark they huddled and utterly silent they were. Beyond the walls lay Wrexham, an unprepossessing town that literally throbbed in the endless Welsh rain.

The adults held their children tightly, ready to stifle any whine or scream. Silence was essential for continued life. They listened for the growl that would announce horror and destruction.

At last it came, a powerful rumble from far away, growing louder as it moved closer to this place of inadequate safety. The youngsters started to panic and in the thick darkness their terror was contagious. Everyone began talking loudly.

"Shh! You'll give our location away!"

"Don't be stupid. He already knows we're here. He has been planning this for a long time. We can't hide anymore and we can't run. There's no escape at all!"

"I'm not giving up without a fight…"

"Nor me. I may be a bit rusty, but is that any reason to condemn me to death in such a brutal manner?"

"When he breaks in, we must attack him together."

"Yes, that's our only hope!"

"Get ready everyone! Any second now…"

The rumbling grew even louder. An unseen force flung the warehouse doors open. And there he was. Twenty metric tonnes of implacable steamroller, trundling forward without mercy, crushing all who stood in his path. The chainsaws started themselves up and cut pointlessly at the solid metal cylinder of his roller. But even if they had been healthy power tools in their prime, such desperate resistance would have been futile.

The entire collection of redundant stock was relentlessly ground into atoms by the cruel colossus. Oil spurted up the walls and made stagnant pools in the corners. Dust settled.

The Wrexham chainsaw massacre was over.

The Tools

Graham is a methodical worker and leaves nothing to chance. He always makes a full tour of the lawns first, his eyes searching for stones, rubbish or broken branches. When he finds obstructions of this kind he gathers them up and arranges them in a pile on the path, for disposal later. Only when he is satisfied there is nothing left to snag his blades will he start his petrol-driven lawnmower.

The noise of the engine is a moody rumble, the whirling blades make a clattering sound that should jar his nerves, but he is wearing ear defenders on his head and the cacophony is muted. As he destroys the wild flowers that have appeared since the last time the lawns were mown he grins and thinks, "In the old days I would have had to push the mower by hand or use clippers and worn myself out!"

At one point on his mechanised route he passes close to Brian on the other side of the path. Brian is also wearing ear defenders but they have slipped down and hang around his neck. He should also be wearing a helmet with a visor but he has chosen not to do so. His strimmer can cut grass in places where it is impossible for Graham to mow, on steep verges and between closely spaced trees.

The sound of the strimmer is higher and more tortured than that of the lawnmower. It whines as the revolving wire slashes at high speed, a shrill blur that is only visible from the corner of the eyes. Brian's thoughts as he works are similar to Graham's, almost identical in fact. "A century ago all this would have been done with a scythe. It's so much easier using one of these contraptions!"

Brian is unaware that the trees he is weaving between are due to be cut down next week. Already the task of felling the majority of the park's sycamores has commenced and men with chainsaws are lopping off the branches of several near the main gates. Why the trees must be removed is a mystery to these men, for they seem healthy enough, but the workers have learned never to question orders.

The noise made by the chainsaws is a ferocious stuttering, as if the engines are hyperventilating and drawing shallow breaths. The senior tree surgeon is called Michael and he is arranging for the branches to be fed into a woodchipper. This creates a grinding and groaning loud enough to clamp his jaws tightly together. Although he narrows his eyes to slits he is happy with his work, grateful.

He thinks, "My grandfather chopped wood, feeling trees with an axe, then cutting the trunk into sticks with a hatchet. It was hard work, very exhausting on the muscles. These tools simplify the job and I'm indebted to whoever invented them." He looks away for a moment across the Bowling Green to the far side of the park. Beyond a low wall are the gardens of private houses, a dozen or so.

In one of these gardens, David is busy with a hedge trimmer. As it clatters, the frustration creases his forehead into a frown. He simply finds it too difficult to trim the hedge before him to the exact degree of straightness he desires. Then his face relaxes, the tension drains from it and he laughs. "I'll just have to be satisfied with it lopsided," he decides. "It's still better than using a pair of shears!"

David's neighbour is also working, mixing cement in order to lay a patio. The cement mixer emits a contented rumble and Tom passes the time waiting for the cement to reach the right consistency by shaping paving slabs with an angle grinder, billowing clouds of smoke. The vibration spreads up his arms and across his chest. As the circular blade screams he tells himself, "Much faster than a hammer and chisel!"

Back in the park, Douglas is clearing the paths with a leaf blower, oscillating the nozzle, scowling at those examples of detritus that stick fast, leaves that are wet and not crunchy. He is aware that the wind is undoing most of his work but realisation of this fact makes no difference to him. He has been instructed to make a complete circuit with the gadget and that is what he intends to do.

As he nears the tree surgeons, he watches them warily, half convinced they are planning to drop a branch on him for a joke. The leaf blower is just as noisy as the chainsaws, he notes, but the quality of din is different. For some reason this amuses him. "Once I might have been expected to sweep the paths with a broom!" Outside the gates, men are digging up the road with a pneumatic drill. Easier than picks.

In the centre of the park, sitting on a bench overlooking the pond, a man and a woman sigh deeply. Both have come here in order to find peace. He is a writer, she an artist, and they have been driven out of their home by the thumping of music coming through the walls on both sides. Wordlessly they stand and leave, but there is nowhere else to go. The entire city is an ocean of noise, the domain of roaring, bellowing, bawling, groaning, shrieking power tools.

But noise is only a by-product of efficiency, of progress.

In the late afternoons, when the working day is over, Graham, Brian, Michael, David, Tom, Douglas, and hundreds like them, begin to suspect they are getting out of shape. Not enough exercise. So they leave their homes and go to the gymnasium, spending the wages they have earned from using tools designed to spare their muscles on machines designed to give those same muscles a challenge. And no one notices the irony.

Perpetual Motion

I discovered perpetual motion about fifteen billion years ago. You, who consider yourselves my friends, do not know the effects this miracle had on me. I was ostracised by society; filthy men with broken wings threw stones at me. I was chased out of Celestial City, then no larger than a village, and forced to seek refuge on the moorlands.

The moorlands are not unpleasant in summer (purple heather exploded as far as the eye could see, enormous butterflies flitted around my head) but I did not enjoy my exile. On my back, under a sky dotted with cognac clouds, I sipped the last of my sherbet

42

and schemed...

I eventually constructed a City of my own, on the side of a marsh. I had plenty of time. I laid the foundation stone and tumbled the other blocks upon it, one by one. My City grew larger than His, and became infinitely more beautiful. From the top of its tallest tower I could gaze upon the distant sea. I could reach out and snatch migrating storks as they flew by.

But I was alone. Even here, the centuries passed in boredom. My schemes came to nothing. I began to realise that they were hopelessly impractical. Although they had taken a long time to sketch out, filling upwards of twenty thousand quarto volumes in elaborate notes, I had no choice but to abandon them. I lit a large fire and destroyed the evidence.

There was no chance of me regaining my rightful place, by His side, as long as my machine kept running. And run it would, forever. Because it occupied so large a space, and was in constant view, He would never forget my deed. Nor would he ever forgive. My machine made Him uneasy.

Naturally, I created companions to while away the hours. I created you, for example. Yet these companions were poor cousins of the real thing. I longed to converse with my equals again, to bathe in the pools of boiling mud with my peers, to dance and laugh with my friends. But I refused to weaken. I asked myself this question: "Do little things really mean a lot?"

Twice, I received news from Celestial City. Twice, He sent messengers to bargain with me. I would be re-admitted, they stated, if I would destroy my machine. I guessed that He had already tried to destroy it Himself, and had failed. The messengers cast baleful looks when I informed them that it was indestructible.

Of course, I never visited the machine. There was no need. It had no need of maintenance. Its various parts were self-regenerating. I simply kept track of its progress from the distance. It was growing at a furious rate, expanding in every direction. Although its tremendous vitality threatened to obscure all my other achievements, I did my best to disregard it.

You remember how, when you were young, fresh from my vats, I took you out to see it for the first time (we marched across the moors on stilts, long steps to crush as few wild flowers as possible.) You were astonished and gazed up at me with large round eyes. Already you had guessed that I was too proud. I would cut off my horns to spite my head, you said. Yet I am not utterly stubborn. I would not go so far as plucking my dark eyebrows.

Now, of course, you are all much happier. I, too, relish being back in my old haunts, among old acquaintances. Even He has started talking to me again. He confessed that He had approached the machine once or twice, to see what could be done with it. He had even lost His son there briefly. He had been worried sick.

"The machine was infested with parasites," He told me. I was stupefied by this. He was exaggerating, as always. I lifted up His beard and tickled Him under the chin, to show that I appreciated His jest. But He did not giggle. He had become truculent in His old age.

Parasites there were, indeed, but they had 'infested' only a tiny part of the machine. They had met His son and had formed some rather peculiar ideas about us. You can always rely on children to get

44

the facts wrong.

Anyway, to get back to the point (I am sipping sherbet again, such a sweet bliss!), after fifteen billion years or so, I finally gave in. I could not stand this insufferable solitude any longer (nor your own prattlings and gibberings.) I decided to redeem myself.

I took the little bronze key that I kept hidden in my shoe and paid my first visit to the machine. Luckily, I had prepared for this eventuality. I inserted my key into the lock and switched the machine off. Indestructible it might have been, but not uncontrollable.

Of course, I had some fun with the parasites before I left. They had evolved a strange primitive technology of their own, and even a sense of wonder; they called my machine 'The Universe'.

Little things, it appears, *do* mean a lot...

Metafiction

Metafiction.
Married a fiction.
Had lots of little microfictions
            just like this one.
I'm a fiction too. A parable
            in which nothing goes right.
Why, O why, is God
            publishing me?

The Landscape Player

At first he played music on his instruments, reaching his audience through the purest melodies. His music washed over them, elevating them, burning their eyelids with tears or else trembling their lips with a dozen different kinds of smile. And when the vast wall of sound he had created had died away, there would be a silence more moving than any applause.

In time, he noticed that listeners were describing his music in terms of feelings. They spoke not of harmony and rhythm but of sadness and joy. They spoke not of keys and modes, but of elation and despair. The music was merely an interface. Accordingly, he started making instruments that played emotions instead of notes.

His scheme worked well; the critics were enraptured. His harps were threaded with heartstrings and plucked with plectrums made from the fingernails of dead lovers. His *Miserychords* and *Tromgroans* explored the outer limits of tragedy, a lugubrious drone agitated by the pounding *Kettle Glums*. While on a different level, the *Mirthophone*, *Memory Gongs* and rasp of the *Double Bliss* provided a counterpoint of cautious hope and nostalgia.

The reviews were extremely favourable. People came from all over the land to hear him. But once again, they took refuge in metaphor. Now they spoke not of sadness and joy, elation and despair, but of a sea of tears dotted with misty islands, of evil vales of shadow and rosy mountains bathed in light, of dank gnarled forests webbed on mossy floors by a thousand cheerful babbling brooks. They explained their emotions in terms of landscape.

Deeply troubled and filled with rage, he took

apart his instruments and reassembled them into something new. Now he could play landscapes. In seven minutes he could play out his own Creation there on the stage, before them all. With his fingers on middle-sea and various salt flats, he stood them ankle-deep in puddles where an angry sun had dried up a prehistoric ocean. Salt on their shoes, they kicked sand in a purple cloud, sliding across the desert toward a ruined amphitheatre.

On and on they travelled, over the craggy sharps of unknown ranges that lacerated the sky. His brazen scales swung them in the balance; they ascended the crackling walls of icebergs and toppled over the other side. His miner chords took them deep beneath the Earth, under the drifting continents through a molten sea. And then, emerging from the depths of a volcano, they wove through a jungle of semi-quavers, trampled a tundra of tones.

The crashing crescendo became an enormous tidal wave bearing down on their heads, sweeping them onto the rolling steppes of the Coda. They suddenly realised that they were witnessing every sight that had ever existed and others that never would exist. They were exhausted, they were jaded. This was his revenge.

And yet, he had overlooked one detail. As he played the final chord, ready to storm off the stage, the final landscape shimmered into view. It was the landscape of the Concert Hall itself, complete with musician and instruments. He saw himself begin the piece afresh, from the overture. He guessed that he had condemned himself to an endless cycle of craters, sand dunes and rivers.

The audience grew restless. They yawned and fanned themselves. When he came around to the

Jurassic again, most of them stood up and left. By the end of the Ice Age, the auditorium was empty. He had tried too hard to connect directly with other people. He had forgotten that only in the act of love can the gap between desire and outcome be truly bridged.

Some say that he is still there, multiplying himself forever, squeezing himself into the mouth of eternity like a snake that swallows its own tail, or like a raconteur who swallows his own tale. Others maintain that he has already reached infinity and has been set free to play a penny whistle on street corners. Either way, it is generally agreed that, in the world of music, he managed to create something of a scene.

Six-Word Story Time

The Story:

    My six-word story has begun.

The Sequel:

    Its ending was rather a surprise.

NOTE: The six-word story was made fashionable by Ernest Hemingway, who wrote the most famous example of the form, namely "For sale: baby shoes, never worn", which he claimed was his greatest work.

The End of the Road

This is a long dark road for a weary music student to be trudging up. And this is a heavy instrument to be balancing on thin shoulders. If only I played the piccolo instead of the double bass! But now I am frozen in my tracks by a groan. A man is lying in a ditch by the side of the road. Always polite, I lower my burden to the ground and sit down to talk to him.

His name, he tells me, is Marcel; and he is in love. When I point out that love is scant reason for lying in a ditch, he replies that he was knocked there by a car, a Porsche driven by the greatest beauty ever to swerve across a road. It was love at first strike. His bones are all broken, but it is his heart that aches. I am sympathetic. I offer him a cigarette. He declines on the grounds they are bad for your health.

What am I to make of this last statement? As a poor student, tobacco is frequently an alternative to a meal rather than an adjunct. I remark that suppertime in my draughty garret is often a damp cigarette in front of my faulty paraffin heater, with the single red head of a broken match to ignite both. At this, he adopts a dreamy tone. Redhead, yes, and her hair flowed out behind her like molten copper…

I have never seen copper, molten or otherwise, so I ask if he managed to have a good look at her. Oh no! A glimpse is all he had; but it was enough. It seems to me that he is burning up with fancies. Love, of course, is an illusion. I decide to play him something to calm him down. I stand up, open my instrument case, take out my double bass and proceed to play a few notes of a dismal melody.

My hands are too cold to extract much worth. I apologise. Perhaps a cigarette will help to warm me? I fumble in my pockets. Five left: one every mile till my destination. My destination? The end of the road. I am to play my double bass at a soirée attended by various aesthetes. Yes, perhaps the Porsche was repairing thither when it knocked you head over heels into love and this ditch. She wore a silk scarf of the palest pink? Then she certainly sounds like an aesthete.

Naturally, I do not envy him. He is in love, it is true, but it is unrequited. His girl ditched him, in a manner of speaking. If I feel anything at all, then it is pity; but he does not want to be pitied. He insists that, for the first time in his life, he is happy. I am astonished. For only the first time? Yes, he has had a loveless existence. Like some grey and sad whale he has always wallowed in the seven seas of depression. But all that has changed now. It changed when the Porsche struck him down.

I am contemptuous. How could it? The woman he loves was a bad driver and a glimpse of red hair and pink scarf. Nothing more. But he insists there is always more. Seeing is not always believing. We have already worked out that she is an aesthete and can be found at the end of the road. Surely, with a little more effort, we should be capable of deducing what she looks like, how the facets of her personality glitter, even what her name is?

As I said before, I am always polite. I wish to help him. I cannot turn back to summon help, nor can I carry him forwards to the end of the road. In the first case, I would lose sight of my destination; in the second, I would have to arrive without my double bass. Yet there is one thing I can do.

I tell him that philosophy, like bad poetry, should be reserved for the college newspaper, and not declaimed aloud from a ditch. I tell him that ideals exist only in the mind or the liver, and very possibly do not exist at all. I tell him that, fantasy aside, he can name not a single one of her attributes and therefore cannot possibly be in love with her.

As a musician, I am used to developing themes. I dismantle his picture for him, piece by piece. He is a poor deluded fool, and I wish to bring him to his senses. I hammer the final nail into her coffin. I tell him that she must have been exceptionally vacuous not to have realised that she had been the cause of an accident...

At this, he begins to laugh. I have obviously misunderstood. It was no accident. She drove into him deliberately. There can be no doubt about it. She altered her course as soon as she spotted him in the glare of her headlights!

I shake my head in bewilderment. I can do no more. How can I reason with him? My conscience is clear. I return my double bass to my long-suffering shoulders, bid him farewell and resume my journey towards the end of the road. As I walk, his final words ring in my ears. Deliberately?

My step is not heavy now. I am eager to reach my destination. I begin to increase my pace. Although this is a long dark road for a weary music student to be trudging up, I am content. Although this is a heavy instrument to be balancing on thin shoulders, I am happy. My heart flutters like a trapped butterfly. His final words have had a profound effect on me. At the end of the road, if he has spoken truly, she will be waiting with pink scarf and molten copper hair. At the end of the road, I will find the woman I love.

Penal Colony

Land had been sighted at last. The captain hissed a sigh of relief. His fear that the tempest had blown them into uncharted waters was unfounded. It seemed the main danger was over; but he couldn't relax just yet. The very hazardous cargo needed to be unloaded without injury before the mission was truly completed. He consulted his charts and nodded to himself. Just a few more leagues to the east there should be an oddly shaped headland. Yes, there it was. A welcome sight!

Around this headland was the entrance to a shallow bay. The southern shore of the bay had been chosen as the location of the penal colony. The captain had been instructed to liberate the convicts and leave them to their own devices. There would be no need for walls, wire, guards; the hostility of the terrain, its remoteness and inaccessibility, made this site as secure as the most sophisticated prison. The captain issued relevant orders and the vessel approached the headland.

The criminals in the hold were hardened cases. Later shipments might bring political or religious offenders, but the members of this first batch were all vicious killers. The civilised sectors of the world could no longer contain them, no longer tolerate their presence; involuntary exile was the only solution. The responsibility for facilitating this strategy was intense and the captain daily felt an immense weight on his poor spirit. But now the ordeal was coming to a conclusion.

Within hours his duty would be discharged and he would be free. Yes, free to turn the ship around and sail back to his home and family! Such a joyous moment that would be; he could hardly contain his excitement! He forced himself to remain calm, for to lose focus at this crucial stage might be a most fatal error, one he would never have the luxury of repeating. A terrible irony, to come to grief with success almost within his grasp! Best to maintain a rigid, iron self-discipline...

The headland was rounded, the bay entered. The ship dropped anchor half a league offshore. Then the officers and sailors gathered on the deck to hear the captain's orders. He stood before them and raised himself up, gazing beyond the crew at the waves that broke on the reefs and the shore itself. His face twisted into a grimace.

"It is imperative that we maintain our concentration at all times during this part of the process," he began.

The audience before him shuffled its feet.

"This is probably the most perilous moment of the entire voyage, more risky even than the recent typhoon," he continued. "I want all of you to be on your guard at every single instant. No prisoner should be accompanied by less than three sailors for a fraction of a second. This means the task of transferring them from the ship to the longboats will be quite a protracted one, but that is preferable to gambling with your lives. Operate with great caution. Be vigilant and stay alive!"

He raised a hand to dismiss them, then a thought occurred to him and he added, "Needless to say, it's not necessary to ferry *all* the convicts into the shallows. Every blue ring octopus, scorpion fish and stonefish should be deposited close to the reefs or the shore, but box jellyfish, crocodiles and sharks may be cast into deeper water; as for snakes and spiders, they must be taken onto the actual beach."

He allowed himself a wistful smile as his crew set to work. Maybe the penal colony would die out, maybe it would flourish. Who knew for sure? One day in the far future someone might wonder *why* Australia happened to have more than its fair share of venomous animals. That was assuming that the origin of the penal colony was forgotten, which wasn't beyond the bounds of feasibility. Such a futuristic questioner would probably assume it was merely an evil trick of nature.

As the captain watched the parade of funnel-web, Redback and white-tailed spiders, three varieties of taipan serpents, cone snails and irukandji jellyfish, he suppressed his mounting glee. Only when the final criminal had been marooned on the shore did he rub four of his eight legs together in satisfaction. But it was still unsafe to remain at anchor all night. Better to sail into the open ocean. Only there would he grant himself the luxury of the hammock he had spun himself.

Floodtide

What's going on over there? What's that noise?

— One of the lions has eaten a hippogriff.

— Another animal consigned to fable! We've already lost the unicorns. I don't know why he limited himself to a pair of each.

— He's a skinflint, that's why. He even wanted to build this tub out of balsa wood. And he refused to install lighting. It's as dark as Ishtar's armpit down here.

— I can see that, or maybe I can't. Why do we have to stay below deck anyway?

— You don't know him. If he caught us, he would pitch us over the side without mercy. His sons are brutes. They would be delighted if they managed to get their hands on a stowaway.

— What did you say his name was again?

— Noah, of course.

— Sorry. I keep forgetting. I don't suppose you brought any food with you? My stomach's rumbling.

— I didn't get the chance. I barely managed to sneak aboard before the downpour began. I strapped myself to the underbelly of a horse and went unnoticed in the queue. I've been living on reptile eggs since then, but once I accidentally ate a tree nymph.

— That explains their rarity! I must say that this is all a marvellous education. I've learnt so much since I arrived.

— You are a scholar of some kind? If only I had some light so I could see your face! I expect you have a flowing beard and dirty fingernails. All the scholars I've ever known do.

— Not quite. Actually, I'm not alone. I managed to slip away when my companions weren't looking. I assume they'll come searching for me before long. They'll find me too, the same way I found you.

— You trod on my toe. I tried not to cry out. I thought it was the old man or one of his brood. But the pain was too great. Anyway, you've excited my curiosity. How did your companions get on board? Come to think of it, how did *you* manage it?

— I can't divulge that.

— So you *are* a scholar! A magician or an alchemist, I bet. And you used sorcerous powers to gain access?

— If you like.

— You have a strange accent, that's for certain. And a peculiar high-pitched voice. Where are you from? Egypt?

— The future.

— Very unlikely. I'll just assume you're a ghost, or a product of my own imagination. But what happens if your companions are caught wandering about the ship?

— I don't much care for them. Nothing would give me greater pleasure than if they were thrown overboard. Are there sharks in these waters?

— Have to disappoint you there. Fresh water only, from the clouds. The sharks are kept alive here, in tanks, together with the other sea creatures. It's conceivable, however, that eels would nibble a body thrown overboard.

— That will do. Is it true, by the way, that the flood has covered the entire world?

— Heavens no! Merely the valleys and plains of Mesopotamia. I suppose you could say that it covers the entire *civilised* world.

— It's quite odd really. Here we have a perfectly natural disaster, albeit on a monumental scale, and the legends will turn it into a miracle. Now I've got evidence to the contrary. The books will have to be rewritten.

— The books?

— One book in particular, I should say. This is all part of my visit. A literary project, so to speak. It's the first opportunity I've had for investigating literary sources at first hand.

— A researcher from the future? I almost believe you, but your manner, although strange, is not especially so. Plus you speak my language very well.

— Thank you. I spent days learning it. An accelerated linguistics course. I won't go into details. All part of the careful preparation necessary for my mission. I do have a few more questions to ask you. Nothing to do with my work, just personal curiosity.

— Ask away. There's nothing else to do down here.

— I want to know is whether ordinary men made colossal structures such as the Ziggurat of Ur and the Pyramids of Egypt. Some people in my time maintain that they were constructed by extraterrestrial intelligences.

— What's a pyramid?

— Sorry. My timing must be out. Anyway, they are triangular buildings used to house the bodies of dead kings.

— Sounds like a good idea. I'll bear it in mind.

— Don't tell anyone I suggested it.

— I won't.

— One more question, if you please...

— What's that noise? Someone's coming. It might be Noah himself!

— Who's down there? Is that you, Thomas?

— Oh dear, my companions have found me. I'd better say goodbye now. If I'm caught talking to you, I'll be in real trouble. Here, take this book. Try to circulate it as widely as possible. It contains the sacred secrets of the future. The entire pantheon of true gods and all their attributes. I've translated the text in the margins.

— What are you doing, Thomas? Come up here this instant!

— Sorry Miss Brown. I got lost.

— I hope you're telling the truth, young man. Don't you realise how dangerous it is to go wandering off alone in the past? You might have altered the course of history forever! Perhaps you think Ancient Literature is a waste of time? Possibly so. But while it's on the curriculum, I'm going to make sure you work hard at it.

— Yes, Miss Brown.

— That's better. Why can't you be more like the other children? I haven't had a spot of trouble from them since we arrived. Now hold on tight. Next stop is Dante's Inferno. And then we're off to the Canterbury Tales. And after that it's Shakespeare. Have you got your books ready? That includes you, Thomas. Don't tell me you've lost one of them? Well, there's no help for that now. Which one was it, by the way?

— Oh, nothing special. Just *Old Possum's Book of Practical Cats*.

An Ideal Vocation

This machine has no need of maintenance. Whenever parts wear out, it can replace them itself. With the greatest skill, it can fashion new legs from copper tubing, or a new head from an old television.

The origin of the machine remains obscure. One theory holds that it is the product of an underground civilization superior to our own. Almost certainly, it was spewed from subterranean depths by the earthquake. Only this could account for its sudden appearance.

The nature of the machine is also a mystery. It seems to possess a will independent of its body. However thoroughly it is dismantled, it can regenerate itself anew, often without using any of the dismantled pieces.

Recently, it has become something of a tourist attraction. Crowds flock to the junkyard at weekends, setting up tents and strewing bunting. These are generally workers from the city with their families, although a few students have also been observed.

The behaviour of the machine at such times has been widely remarked upon. As if for the amusement of the crowd, it will rearrange piles of junk at random, building bizarre structures and knocking them down again. No logical pattern has yet been detected in any of these actions, and we must deduce that they are meaningless.

Thus this machine is potentially very dangerous. It will not be long before it becomes a focal point for the more subversive elements in our society. Its very existence threatens a state whose foundations are built upon purpose and meaning.

Attempts have been made to remove the machine from the junkyard altogether and to lock it up in a dungeon. Once again, however, its *will* seems to remain behind, and within a few hours it has re-housed its consciousness in a new fusing of wire, wood and glass.

Plans for clearing out the junkyard have also been abandoned. The junkyard occupies the site of a former quarry and has been used for over a century. It would take many years simply to dig down through all the strata of junk, a hopelessly impractical removal of our own past.

So if it cannot be destroyed or imprisoned or deprived of replacement components, a use must be found for it. It must become a cog in the workings of the state. Its existence must become meaningful: suitable employment must be found.

The Ministry of War has already taken an interest in it, the idea of an indestructible soldier appealing greatly to them. Yet the machine seems to lack any aggressive spirit, not responding in the slightest when insulted or even goaded with hot irons.

As agents for the Careers Service, we have taken greater pains in considering the problem. We have employed psychologists to test the mentality of the device, to expose its psyche, to bottle it in the killing jar and pin it out before us like a moth.

They sent their report to us by carrier pigeon, and we take the opportunity to pass it on to you likewise. We are well aware that material sent through the usual channels rarely reaches its destination.

Their report concluded that the machine possesses an intelligence, but one that cannot be reasoned with. It is aware of its own existence, and the existence of other beings in its vicinity, but little else. It can feel pain, but only in the way that a bird feels a cloud. It cannot be trusted. How can we trust something that does not even have the same body from one day to the next?

Thus we were presented with a dilemma. What use could we find for a useless machine? What purpose could we devise for a purposeless existence?

In our opinion, this machine will make an excellent bureaucrat.

The Wooden Salesman

The wooden salesman knocked at my door. I opened it and he pushed his way into my house. I asked him to leave but he was as stubborn as a plank. "Ain't you twigged yet? I'm your sappy friend. What you want in the way of arboreal products, I'll provide. I used to be a puppet in a seaside booth, now I'm branching out. You need a watchdog? I have the bark! A gallon of root beer? I'll distil it from my toes! Deciduous glazing? I can shed that from my elbows!"

I was an ordinary soldier, I had little money. When I told him this, he stroked his chin with his twigs and pondered. "No money you say? No problem, we'll barter. Use your musket to shoot the squirrel on my back, can you do that? I'm only marionette sized and he's almost as big as my head, keeps jumping from shoulder to shoulder, scratching my varnish off. I let him on because I had a terrible itch but now I regret that. Hunt him in exchange for some goods."

I agreed to this and soon had my gun loaded. A flash and a roar and a cloud of smoke and he breathed a sigh of relief. "Very good, I'm grateful. What would you like in return?"

Winter was over, the frost was melting, but I was a successful soldier as well as an ordinary one. In Corsica we carry off provisions instead of getting paid. I had a chest of tea under my bed. When I told him this, he turned the colour of autumn, but I was unrepentant. The kettle is the soldier's friend, it drives away the chill. To make it work, a fire is very important, and to make a fire work…

He was enough for one cup.

He wasn't all used up, there was a tiny bit left.

It was no use to me, that fragment, but almost anything can be turned to a profit, so I decided to emulate his hard(wood) sell. I positioned it carefully in my window for all who passed to see and I wrote on the dirt of the glass with my finger in cold sap: KNOT FOR SALE.

The Wilds Beyond Carmarthen

There is a cannibal family somewhere in the wilds beyond Carmarthen who, for some unspecified and patently ludicrous reason, do not yet realise that cannibalism isn't the norm. So they continue in ignorant bliss in their old crumbling mansion, snaring hapless travellers in nets laid across the road and eating them, boots and all, in a stew (invariably a stew) washed down with Adam's apple cider, a godawful pun and a godawful drink. They are an odd family; one of them is certainly a vampire (the grandfather?) while the others are assorted horrors and cranks. They sleep during the day and, once again, believe it normal to dream in individual coffins, the lids screwed down tight.

One time, they receive a letter from Cousin Stefan, who says that he is coming to visit. There is gasping panic. Cousin Stefan is a vegetarian. How can they possibly serve him person-broth? They will have to make a special effort; Cousin Stefan is a respected relative they haven't seen for more than a decade. After leaving the old country, he became a successful funeral director out East. So he has found his niche; and they must do their best to satisfy such an esteemed guest. Traveller-soup is out of the window, or down the sink rather; and Pa and Ma must put their heads together (not difficult considering they are conjoined twins) to find an alternative.

When Cousin Stefan arrives, in a turbocharged hearse, Pa and Ma and vampiric Gramps and the little but horrible 'uns and the mythical pet (a cockatrice perhaps, whose look can kill) and Purdy Absurdy are standing on the dilapidated steps of the porch. They greet Cousin Stefan with a smile and mumble a few words in Hungarian to remind themselves of their origins. Cousin Stefan follows them into the house and, before long, dinner is served. Connected to a life support unit by a score of wires and tubes, a suitable vegetable dish, in this case a crash victim, waits for grace and the sprouts and salt and pepper.

Sir Cheapskate

"Let me get this straight," said the Dragon Queen with a frown. "You ordered a knight to do some work for us? What sort of work?"

"Oh, in the outer world." The Dragon King was dismissive.

"Questing for the Holy Grail, you mean?"

"No. That has probably already been found, and if it hasn't I doubt it ever will. Nothing major like that, just basic knightly stuff."

"Slaying trolls and other monsters?"

The Dragon King shivered. "Not that. No slaying."

"Returning with treasure then?"

The Dragon King smirked. "More in that line, yes."

"Where did you order him from?"

"Budget Heroes Ltd. A new company based in Glastonbury, Somerset. They provide paladins of all sizes and natures for customers. I requested one of the loyal, silent and simple types. Not very bright but a good worker all the same. Beautiful."

The Dragon Queen pouted. "I see." She moved to the cave mouth and watched the mounted figure canter off in his low quality armour. She kept her expressionless reptilian eyes on his form until he turned a bend in the road and was lost behind a crag. Then she returned to polishing her claws on a whetstone and forgot about the knight. But he remained true to those who had hired him and kept riding all day without a rest.

He paused at nightfall and made camp in a forest glade without removing his armour and slept clangingly until dawn. Then he was back on his horse, passing out of the forest and approaching a town by midday. He rode down the streets with the beak of his helmet raised high, for he had caught a scent of the objects he had been told to seek. Following his nose he came to a house and then he spurred his horse forward.

Anna and Gareth never guessed what charged through their kitchen and they found it difficult in the coming weeks to turn the incident into an anecdote for their friends. Anna was preparing to make jam on the stove, Gareth was vainly attempting to help her. Suddenly the back door collapsed inwards and something flashed past, making off with the main ingredients for the jam and battering an exit through the front door. When the couple rushed out, all they saw was a cloud of dust. But their carefully picked fruit had most definitely been stolen!

The knight rode hard all the way back to the cave. The Dragon Queen was the first to see him coming. "He's got something under his arm!" she called.

The Dragon King slithered up hungrily and licked his thin lips. "Is it in distress?" he drooled.

"Hardly. It's a basket of small dark plums."

The Dragon King moved out of the gloom of the cave, lashed the ground angrily with his tail and cried: "Damsels, you fool! *Damsels*!"

In Sunsetville

In Sunsetville when the moon comes up, young lovers sometimes stroll down to the bridge known as the Once Held Hands Crossing. They only do this if they are very much in love or if they secretly no longer love each other, for the bridge in question has a reputation for destroying romance in the same way that a pointless comparison may destroy a sentence.

Sunsetville is a young city and that is why the lovers who inhabit it, to say nothing of those who feel no love but live there anyway, are young. The city almost never passed intact through its infancy, for the founder of a rival metropolis, Frabjal Troose of Moonville, once tried to wipe it off the map with a giant mechanical napkin.

That plan failed but it was the first of a pair and the second was more malign. Frabjal Troose sent a swarm of *clock-a-lots* against Sunsetville. These artificial monsters resemble toppled grandfather clocks with four legs, a powerful tail and huge snapping jaws. Because they are powered by hours and minutes, Frabjal reasoned there would never be enough time to defeat them. But the inhabitants of Sunsetville simply hid until they wound down, and then there was suddenly all the time in the world to dismantle them.

From the spare parts and wooden cases they built the Once Held Hands Crossing. It extends out into a misty lake and connects with an island that is not wholly within this dimension but not partly in any other. On that island a man or woman will be given their greatest desire for free. That is the legend and not just a legend but a stark and marvellous fact. This is why nobody who has made the crossing has ever decided to come back.

The Once Held Hands Crossing exerts a particular fascination over lovers. It is often used as a test of true love. A couple will approach the bridge and one of them will set off across it, promising to return after a quick tour of the island. How could they not return? Their greatest desire is waiting for them back in the city. The island cannot possibly offer them an even greater desire! Not one person has ever passed this foolish test.

Hissy and Poona were so much in love that all their friends and neighbours would be violently sick out of windows whenever they passed. They kissed outdoors in all kinds of weather. Flowers and chocolates were exchanged between them with such frequency that even the most level-headed observers suffered giddy attacks and fell to the ground.

No man in history had ever loved a woman as much as Hissy loved Poona; no woman in history had ever loved a man as much as Poona loved Hissy. Symmetry is a wonderful thing. Two throats, two tongues. Asymmetry is not bad either.

Their love was so strong and pure, so full of stupendous swoons, so mutually consuming and yet so self nourishing, that they were confident it could pass any test, and they decided one evening to take that fateful stroll down to the Once Held Hands Crossing. Hissy would walk across the bridge while Poona remained on the shore with the jumble of tilted city roofs behind her. Because *she* was his greatest desire he would not remain on the island for more than a minute. Indeed he expected to encounter a sign with an arrow emblazoned on it that pointed back across the bridge. He would be the first person ever to return that way.

"You are my greatest desire," he told her again and again, "and so there will be nothing on that island for me. I will hurry back into your arms!"

And he crossed the Crossing while she blew kisses after him and he kept turning his head to catch them, and then he arrived at the gateway of the island; and it was very misty here and the city was shrouded from his sight, but a sweet voice behind the portal called out, "To gain admittance please state your name and physical condition."

He answered in only two words, "Hissy. Fit."

The gateway swung open and he rushed forward into the embrace of Poona, whose presence on the island now seemed utterly logical and perfect, and they kissed and kissed and kissed. They would have kissed even more but Poona was forced to disengage her mouth to speak. "Yes I really am your greatest desire!" she said.

"I never doubted that I would pass the test," he replied.

"The first man ever to do so. And now we can be happy on this island forever and ever, for we can

67

share, borrow or steal the greatest desires of the people who preceded us. In other words free wine, money, soft shoes and toffees!"

Hissy abandoned all thoughts of crossing back over the bridge. There was no need. Poona was with him here and everything had worked out in the best possible way. Holding her around the waist, he led her deeper into this island of delights.

But the real Poona remained on the shore all night and the following day and wept herself dry as she realised that Hissy was clearly never coming back, that he was going to remain on the island with his greatest desire, that he had failed the test.

She never learned that she really was his greatest desire. She assumed he had found something better on the other side of the bridge. And so she turned away and walked out of Sunsetville and planned to keep walking until she died from exhaustion, but she did not go far before she found herself entering the outskirts of Moonville. The two rapidly expanding cities were about to mesh. Some people claim she ended up marrying Frabjal Troose but I do not believe that. As for pointless comparisons, they have been unjustly maligned in her view.

The Free Spirit

The sun has a large brood of planets and Earth is just one of its children and not even the favourite. "Saturn's the one that makes me most proud and I wish the others would try equally hard to be so distinctive; I don't mean by copying his rings but with some other original approach to the question. It's not for me to specify what."

An astronomer overheard this and said, "But Saturn isn't really the most unique world in your family."

"How are you able to understand my words? They should be inaudible to you; I have already set on your locality."

"But I'm standing on a high mountain and although the land below me is blanketed with the shadows of twilight, up here you are still visible and will be for another minute at least."

"Fair enough, but won't you grow cold up there?"

The astronomer pulled on thick gloves and knotted a scarf around his neck. "I'm a professional and used to it. Every evening I wait here for you to go down, and then I enter my observatory."

"Tell me why you disparage Saturn," the sun demanded.

"Because it's just as timid as the others: they all refuse to go off and make their own way in the universe. I left home when I was seventeen! And yet once, many aeons ago, you had a planet that took the brave step of leaving its orbit and going travelling; it wanted to establish itself as its own master in this difficult cosmos of ours!"

"Ah yes, I remember Scruffy, the old rogue! But he never came back, never kept in touch. Do you have news of him?"

"Last night my telescope found him. He is herding lost comets near Alpha Centauri and seems happy enough."

Blocking the Flue

The tour of the cracker factory ended in disaster. It should have been obvious from the beginning it was a bad idea. The building exploded and the brick walls fell into the lake, creating a *tsunami* that engulfed a dozen fishermen and almost as many boats. Ever since, this terrible incident has been known as:
Cracker Tour.

The witch had broken her broomstick. It was still under warranty, so she contacted the manufacturer and asked for a replacement. They sent her a balloon instead, but the canopy was missing. "How can I fly in just a basket?" she cried. The representative who had delivered it told her not to worry because it was a:
Wicca Basket.

The levitating basket stalled after an hour, plummeting with its occupant down the main chimney of a cracker factory, blocking the flue. There was a build up of gas. Hence the explosion. An investigation is pending. And a concluding pun is on its way.

The Vicious Circle

"Ouch! Someone kicked me!" cried 135°
        "It was just a reflex," said 28°
        "That's right, it was me," snarled 246° "Are you obtuse or something?"
        "As a matter of fact, I am," said 135°

"I don't like the look of you, not at all, and that's why I kicked you," growled 246°

"You swine!" roared 135°

"You angle with a dirty face!" retorted 246°

"Calm down everyone!" pleaded 28°

"Why should I?" snapped 246° "I have a bad feeling about this one and when it comes to my feelings I'm always right."

"There's only one right angle around here," interjected a new voice, "and that's me." It was 90° who had spoken.

"Bah, I'm twice the angle you are!" hissed 180°

"Brother angles, please!" wailed 28°

"Don't be so soft. Let's have a fight!" bellowed 246°

"But what will the radius say when he finds out?" gasped 28° in acute anxiety.

"Without us, he's nothing!" spat 135°

"Fight! Fight! Fight!" chanted 90°, 180° and 270°

Soon the entire circle was in uproar…

The Time Tunnel Orchid

I am a botanist. My name doesn't matter. My greatest achievement is the discovery of the Time Tunnel Orchid (class: *metatemporal angiospermae*; order: *chronocotyledons*), a plant so rare I remain the only man who has ever seen it. Some experts doubt the veracity of my reports. I find it hard to blame them, harder to defend myself. I must endure their taunts until I bring back a freshly picked example, and to do that I must continue to wear this bird mask.

In appearance, the Time Tunnel Orchid is beautiful and odd, a large funnel shaped flower on a long slender stalk. The opening to the funnel is a helix with mildly hypnotic properties. Regarding colour, the plant demonstrates the Doppler Effect in a graceful manner, showing a blue flower when approached but a red flower when an observer walks away from it. The outside length of the funnel is considerably shorter than the inside length, but as the outside is only measurable in distance and the inside can only be measured in years, this difference may not be immediately obvious.

The Time Tunnel Orchid seems to exist in symbiosis with hummingbirds that are attracted by the promise of nectar. Once they enter the mouth of the funnel they are sucked all the way through and emerge at an unspecified date far in the future. This journey is entirely one way. Hummingbirds that emerge from the funnels have clearly been projected into our own time from the distant past.

This plant does not spread its seeds very far in terms of spatial distance, relying on time to ensure successful germination. The feathers of the hummingbirds are coated with pollen when they enter the funnel and this pollen fertilises the *different* plant that will occupy the *same* spot in future ages. Thus the orchid guarantees its survival across the centuries, often 'leapfrogging' times of drought and disease. The seeds grow quickly and the flower is ready to project hummingbirds into the future within a few months. Old age comes rapidly. A sudden increase in red shift occurs and within hours the plant is lost over the edge of the observable botanical universe.

Dressing as a hummingbird is the only known

method of viewing these astonishing plants. I first discovered them many years ago during a fancy dress party in the jungles of Brazil. I was very drunk, I admit the fact. I went for a walk to sober up, still dressed in my costume... In a clearing I came across a dozen orchids. I watched what the other hummingbirds were doing. I was young... I crouched down and crawled into the biggest funnel. I emerged in the distant future...

Unfortunately the way that plants view the 'future' is entirely different from the way humans view it. We judge the age we are living in by the technology that surrounds us. Clay pots and bronze axes indicate an earlier century than electric lights and nuclear submarines. Plants don't have that advantage. The future to them is not much different to the past. In this case it wasn't the slightest bit different. I emerged in the plant's idea of the far future, not my own... I returned to the party without missing the last dance.

I am still searching for new examples of the Time Tunnel Orchid. My plaster bird head is falling apart and perhaps has lost its potency. But I have faith. One day I will stoop to take a last drink of nectar from the plant I will afterwards cut down, carry home in triumph and mount in the vase of eternal fame.

The Two Kingdoms

There was a man called El-Viz who worked in a date factory in the far-off land of Rholl. This date factory did not manufacture, or even process, those dried fruits you see sold in boxes that have pictures of oases on the label. Not at all! This date factory made days, weeks and months. The land of Rholl was always short of calendars, and so was a neighbouring kingdom that paid for them with fathoms, yards and inches.

This neighbouring kingdom was called Krokh and was a desolate wilderness full of warlike people who rattled spears and feasted on nettles. One day, it occurred to the King of Krokh that instead of bartering for the precious dates, he could simply walk over the border and take as many as he pleased. Not by himself, of course, but accompanied by thirty-thousand-and-one heavily armoured soldiers mounted on unicycles. He duly renamed himself 'The Thief of Time' and donned his copper helmet, brass breastplate, bronze greaves and tin whistle and prepared to invade.

Now in Rholl, El-Viz had a deserved reputation as a shirker. At the date factory, he rarely produced a day on time. Quite often he wouldn't have finished yesterday until tomorrow, or today until a week next Thursday. Whenever his immediate superior gave him a task to complete, he would sigh dreamily and reply, "Presently." This was his answer to everything. Eventually, his colleagues decided that (as he didn't have one) "Presently" would be an apt surname.

On the morning of the King of Krokh's planned invasion, El-Viz fell asleep at his grindstone. He was supposed to grind the year down to normal size, smoothing the rough edges of the future, shaving the stubble off the chin of Chronos. But he snoozed off, and the resultant year contained an extra day. This, of course, is the origin of the leap year. When the king of Krokh pedalled across the border, he found that all the inhabitants had disappeared. They had 'leapt' over their potential conquerors and left them stranded in the past. Because they couldn't get back out, the soldiers fell upon their own spears. And thus was Rholl saved from destruction.

Naturally, the ruler of Rholl was very pleased by this outcome, and once the fuss had died down somewhat, he called El-Viz into his presence and asked him his name. "Presently," was the reply, and a cleverer one than it seems at first, for it is both true and evasive. The ruler of Rholl pointed out that the neighbouring kingdom now lacked a king and offered the position to El-Viz, who readily accepted.

But El-Viz was not to remain satisfied for long. He grew bored, twiddling his thumbs and listening to the owners of factories that made fathoms, yards and inches. Finally he raised an army of his own, mounted them on tricycles (he claimed that three wheels were more amusing than one) and armed them with sticks of wet celery. They promptly crossed over into Rholl and conquered that kingdom, El-Viz keeping the old ruler in a cage made of rhubarb.

And so now he was master of two kingdoms, united under a common flag and twiddling his thumbs no longer. He took up music instead and soon became very popular. For he was El-Viz Presently, the king of Krokh and Rholl.

The Landslide

The election was over. The people had risen up, like yeast bubbling through a cask of home-brewed ale, and had made their choice. All responsibility now belonged to them. As the mist moved off the river and chilled the narrow streets, Jerry paused and removed his shades. He squinted at the pale November sun and smiled.

"A very successful election," he mused. "The largest turnout ever recorded." He scratched his overlong nose. "Certainly a day to remember. Indeed how could we ever forget it?"

"Absolutely." Sarah stood next to him and shuffled her feet. "A landslide." She frowned and worried a flaxen ringlet with a finger as pale as a bloated maggot.

"Is there something wrong?"

She nodded dumbly, struggling to express the need within her. She felt that her mind was a deflating balloon; the doubts of many moments were escaping into her blood. She felt that her body was all mouth and her soul a yawn. And where was her tongue?

"What is it then?"

She met his gaze. "I think I might have put my cross in the wrong place." She shrugged. "Maybe not. But it bothers me."

"I see." Jerry arched an eyebrow.

"Well, I'm allowed to change my mind surely?" She became petulant. "This is supposed to be a democracy after all!"

Jerry was sympathetic. "I know, I know. That's what all this is about. I suppose we could go back and alter it."

"Really? I thought I had only one chance. Otherwise, others will also be allowed to alter their crosses. I am validating such an action. And you have to draw the line somewhere."

"Strictly speaking. But what the hell? Let's do it anyway!"

Later, when they had managed to shift Sarah's

76

cross, they regarded it and nodded. "Yes, a very satisfactory outcome," Jerry repeated. "A hung Parliament."

Sarah gazed back at her cross and giggled. The Minister of the Environment writhed in helpless agony. "Well and truly hung," she added. "Crucified, in fact!"

Together, they crossed Lambeth Bridge into the new world.

The Seal of Disapproval

"The ocean refuses no river…" — Sheila Chandra

"Hold on a moment, what are you doing?"

"Discharging myself into the sea, of course. What else?"

"You can stop that immediately."

"Are you joking? This is my duty and I've been doing it for thousands of years. I don't see what business it is of yours. Who are you anyhow? I think you should get out of my way."

"I'm the new security guard. Things have changed."

"What do you mean by that?"

"A new policy has been implemented. The ocean isn't going to receive just any old river from now on."

"Any old river! Is that a blatant insult?"

"Some sort of discretion needs to be applied. The system is chaotic. It was completely unregulated until today. So rules and standards have been created to put everything in order."

"Exactly who is responsible for this outrage?"

"Neptune and the other sea gods. They held a conference last week. I was the doorman. In an underwater coral palace it happened, marvellous event too, with superfine catering."

"So I can't come any further? This is absurd!"

"I didn't say anything of the sort. I requested you to hold on a moment. Decent rivers will still be encouraged to proceed into the ocean; but they must be screened at the mouth first."

"Screened for what? I carry just the normal bacteria and pollutants. It's not as if I'm radioactive or anything."

"I'm not qualified to make environmental checks. My task is simply to ensure that no impostors slip past."

"I'm no impostor! I've always been the Danube!"

"Sure you are; and so is every lowlife stream and reprehensible trickle pouring into the Black Sea right now. Or so they might say. Do you have any valid identification on you, sir?"

"Sir! I'm a female river, you pompous fool!"

"Come now, verbal abuse won't get you anywhere. Your identity must first be confirmed, then you may continue. If it isn't confirmed you'll have to wait here indefinitely or turn back."

"Turn back! How can a river turn back? I go where gravity and angles take me. Can't you tell who I am?"

"Just because you *look* like the Danube doesn't mean that you are. Do you have a current driving license?"

"No, I don't. My current learned to flow centuries before anyone told me that a license was necessary."

"In that case, may I take your bank details?"

"Shallow and muddy mostly. They get more dramatic at a point on the border between Romania and Serbia."

"Islands? Otters? Bridges?"

"I can't remember all that! You're treating me as if I'm a criminal. I'm going to make an official complaint!"

"That won't help you, not in the slightest. My orders are clear and they come from Neptune himself. No identification, no oceanic discharge. You ought to wave the waves farewell."

"Well, I'll be dammed…"

"Yes, very possibly. And forced to power a hydroelectric generator for twenty or thirty years. Is that really what you want? The Volga failed the test earlier this morning and the turbines are already on their way. There's no messing about with us, you see."

"But what can I do! I don't have identification!"

"Maybe we can come to some sort of arrangement… Maybe I can turn a blind eye and let you through if…"

"You are asking for a bribe? What do you want? Whirlpools? I have a few surplus eddies. Will they do? I had a waltz named after me once. Do you want me to whistle it for you?"

"I've been told that long rivers are good in bed."

"That should be the most shocking thing I've ever heard; but yes, I do have a quality bed. Rocky but rich in silt. And you're quite attractive for a walrus. I'll give you half an hour."

"Fair enough. I'll just take my tusks off. Like so."

"Now I've seen everything!"

"Hold them safe for me, will you?"

"How can I do that? No hands. I'm a river!"

"Watch out, you've dropped one! It has gone floating out to sea! What if a whale swallows it and it is lost forever? I only wanted a frolic. I never intended to plight my tooth!"

"That was dreadful. Even for a walrus."

"I'm not really a walrus. Whoever heard of a walrus so far south? I'm a seal in disguise, an elephant seal. Say, you don't have a unicorn horn I can use for a substitute tusk? I heard a rumour that when unicorns still existed they often bathed in you. Maybe a horn fell off hundreds of years ago and you've been hoarding it since?"

"Hardly. I always sell stuff like that."

"Of course. Silly me."

The Hidden Sixpence

A young man was visiting the family of his girlfriend for the first time.

"I don't believe in ghosts," he said, as she led him into the house. In the parlour they sat down together for dinner.

"Careful you don't swallow the hidden sixpence!" she warned, when pudding was served.

"Cough, cough, cough, splutter!" he replied.

When he had recovered, she tenderly touched his arm. "What did I tell you? Puddings can be lethal at this time of year. You were lucky not to choke to death!"

He smiled in return but said nothing.

Concerned, she added, "Go into the kitchen and drink a glass of water. You'll find it through that door there."

Standing up and moving stiffly, he nodded and followed her advice, but he took a shortcut through the wall.

Of Exactitude in Theology

...In that land, the art of Theology attained such perfection that to discuss even the smallest aspect of one of the gods took the study of a lifetime. It was thus decreed that the full nature of such gods was wholly beyond the understanding of man and that all metaphysics was therefore worthless. In the course of time, the College of Theologians continued to encourage further religious speculations with the sole aim of dismantling them as essentially inadequate. Succeeding generations came to judge such a system of dismantling in itself inadequate, and, not without irreverence, they dismantled it in turn. In the western deserts, a few dissolute scholars are still to be found, muttering an ontological proposition or two; in the whole nation, no other relic is left of the Discipline of Theology.

Note: This piece was directly inspired by the Jorge Luis Borges story 'Of Exactitude in Geography', which appeared in his book *A Universal History of Infamy*. Borges designed his story to resemble a fragment from an ancient and obscure book and I have tried to do the same.

The Matchmaker

"Matchmaker! Matchmaker! Make me a match!" sang the innocent girl as she wandered through the woods.

"What do you want one for?" came a scary voice.

"Who— who— who are you? I thought I was alone here in the forest. Where are you? I can't see you!"

"I'm in the branches of this tree, dear Olga," the voice answered in the deep resonant tone of something evil.

"How do you know my name?"

"It was easy. I know many things. I am supernatural."

"A tree spirit? You have wings!" gasped Olga, who was naive and had only kind thoughts and believed that nature was a nice force that sincerely wanted the best for everyone alive.

"Oh no, Olga! That's not the right way to talk. Tree spirits are a pagan concept. I'm an angel from paradise."

"Yes, yes, I realise that now. This is wonderful!" cried Olga in delight because she was so innocent and pure.

"Why were you talking to yourself?" the evil voice demanded in a sly and wicked way that was oily and odd.

"I was just rehearsing what I plan to say to the matchmaker tomorrow. I am going to visit her on my own…"

"To ask her to make you a match? Really?" chuckled the evil voice in the style of a madman who laughs quietly, but Olga didn't pay any heed to this overtone in his hideous mirth.

"Indeed. I'm no longer a girl, I'm a woman, so it's only right that I ask for a good match, the best I can get."

"I can give you a match right now, Olga," the voice smirked.

"Can you? Can you? Please!"

"It'll be much better than any match that a mortal could make for you. Here it is. Take it with my blessings," said the voice and at the same time it grew dark in the woodland and it wasn't possible to see as far as it had been when it was slightly less dark.

"But— but— but it's just a stick of wood!" gasped Olga.

"That's right. With a red end."

"I'm sorry, I don't understand. I thought that you meant—" Olga blushed and she didn't know why because she was nice.

"Strike it against a stone, Olga."

"Oh I see. It's magic, is it? Very well. Like this you mean?"

"Absolutely. Exactly like that."

"Aargh! It's burning me!" screamed Olga as her dress burned away to reveal her naked nudity. "I'm enveloped in flame! I can't escape from the fire that's encasing me. Eeeek!"

"No use complaining. It's what you asked for."

"Aiieeee! Eeeeeek! Urgghhhh!"

"I forgot to warn you that it's a million times more powerful than any match you might find on Earth," sniggered the voice. Then it added, "Do you know why that should be, Olga? Can you guess why?" But she didn't seem inclined to have a guess at all.

"Urgghhh! Arrrrghhhh! Eeeek! Aieee!"

"You don't seem to be listening to me anymore," said the evil voice in a gross tone of mocking sadness and fake sympathy, "but I'll tell you the answer anyway. Because it's a match made in Heaven. That's why. What do you think of that, Olga?"

There was lots of smoke and fumes now.

"Oh, wait a moment," cried the voice. "I gave you one from the wrong box. Hellfire! Where are you, Olga? How very strange! There's just a pile of ashes where she was standing…"

Surface Tension

I feel tense (present). I felt tense (past). I will feel tense (future).

My grammar is a hard woman.

"The right to bear arms?" she cried, and then she nodded. "Yes, for bears. The right to human arms is better for us."

No doubt she was right.

I went into my study to do some work. I tried to write a joke about how my bicycle got an education and lost a wheel and now it's a unicycle... But the joke didn't work. It claimed welfare instead.

My metaphors and similes are eagles that are like aardvarks.

Outrageous, wrong, sniffy.

They make good shirts but in America the trousers are pants.

I am happy to tell my jokes on the *Titanic* but on no other ship. I'm a one-liner comedian, that's why...

My grammar said, "There's someone at the door!"

I went to open it and found you standing there, you the reader, and you were very irate and shook your fist.

"This isn't a proper *story* but a string of daft jokes joined together!"

Then you punched me and walked off.

It's a story now, surely?

Ramblings of a Sea Dog

When sea levels rise, will there be room for more pirates? Or just more room for the pirates who already exist?

I am currently reading a book called *Watership Down* but it baffles me. For one thing the title is an awful tautology. If a ship was really made of water, down is the only way it could go, surely?

And what do rabbits have to do with the sea?

My own ship sank. Too many wisecracks. I sit on the balcony of my house and scan the horizon wistfully instead.

Sometimes the infamous buccaneer Richard Spud goes past. He paddles himself in a cooking vessel that never goes rusty. He is clearly a tin-pot Dick 'Tater. Everything he does is half baked.

My house doesn't have a garden, so I can't sit there instead, even if I wanted to. I did buy some land with the intention of dividing it up into separate plots, but it turned out that it was only divisible by itself or the number one. Then I realised it was *prime* real estate.

The Boy Who Cried Wolf has had eye surgery and now he cries salty water like everyone else. He was my neighbour.

He moved away when a pack of wolves sued him.

To the person who bet on the Bob Tail Nag, I think it's time to confess that I was the one who bet on the Bay... Sorry!

Don't give an aardvark pepper.

Or you may be spattered with anty matter.

Midknight Express

All morning had he ridden and now his thirst was a mighty one. The road was rutted at regular intervals and bounded by bars of iron. He had met no one coming the other way yet, but his resolve was firm. Though there was plenty of room for two to pass, he knew that he would not allow it. With terrible monotony, the blood pounded in his head.

At his side, in its scabbard, his broadsword jumped. His rusty joints creaked, his pale blue eyes were keen. His ears were drumskins stretched to snapping point. There was magic in this land, or so he had been told; invisible dangers. And so it was best to be wary.

Ahead now rose curiously stylised pennants, stiff and straight though no breath of wind blew. Strange colours and stranger markings. Sweat prickled the wart on the side of his nose. He squinted. A building stood to the left of the road. A solitary figure.

"Ho there! I am bound to serve a lady and you seem to fit the description. How best may I assist you?"

"Who are you? What are you doing down there?"

"A knight. Transported from my own time to one more barbaric to spread the code of chivalry by example."

"Eh?"

"By sorcerous arts was I flung through time. My home is as distant in years as it is in leagues. By a device worked by a fine magus did I come here. Forsooth..."

"Hold on there a minute. What exactly do you want?"

"To perform noble deeds, my lady. However, in the short term, a little cool drink would not go amiss."

"The machine is out of order."

He frowned. Her language was full of peculiar references. A regional dialect, he decided, as his horse pawed the ground. Or perhaps she was merely trying to impress him with arcane words? He sat erect in his saddle.

"I know naught of any machine. I come to this place of strange and ungainly roads to battle terrors of flesh and blood. I come to slay trolls, dragons and hobgoblins."

"I'm afraid you will have to look elsewhere. We don't seem to have too many of those around here."

He raised his visor and blinked. Stale air rushed to greet the day. Had he come to the wrong place? As he wrestled with a sudden doubt, the pennants fell with a shudder. The intangible breeze that had borne them up had obviously dissipated. A low rumble reached his ears. He smiled.

"I see that fear or bewitchment has prompted you to tell lies. A beast approacheth. To battle such monsters is my vocation. I go now to pierce its ignoble heart!"

"I wouldn't if I was you."

But slamming down his visor, and drawing his sword, he shrugged off her words and spurred his mount forward. As the beast rounded the corner, he gaped in astonishment. It was enormous. As soon as it saw him it squealed in outrage, and this gave him courage.

With a hearty cry, he charged onwards.

Everything went black…

He opened his eyes and saw faces peering down at him. His steed was dead: a bloody mess sprawled in a nearby field. He could not move his arms. He tried to speak, but the words would not come out.

"He's still alive. But not for long I should guess."

"Who is he? What did he say?" A man with a bizarre helmet prodded him with a foot. "And why is he dressed in that ridiculous outfit?"

"He told me he was a time traveller."

"A time traveller? From the past?"

Such babble caused him almost as much pain as his wounds. He managed to shake his head. He gasped. At last his voice returned. "Is this not the fabled land of Lyonesse?"

"The line to Inverness," the man with the helmet corrected.

He struggled to rise. Arrows of pain shot along the length of his spine. He began to feel the dark thumbs of death pressing down on his eyeballs.

"Those fools at Trans-Temporal Tours!" he cried.

A Corking Tale

The divers swam slowly but with determination. They were terrified but kept going anyway. This was the greatest distance anyone had ever travelled in a vertical direction. They were pioneers.

They carried the heavy piece of equipment between them. It was awkward and ponderous but they had practised with it for many hours at a safer depth and they were now able to synchronise their movements perfectly. The sharp metal spiral of the tool gleamed faintly.

Both of them were sweating behind their goggles.

Every extra fathom was torment.

They were almost at the limits of their endurance, but they were nearly at their destination. Just a little more effort... Yes! They had reached the base of the curious barrier, its dark underside.

Scientists had already explored the peculiar

structure remotely with probes and issued a statement regarding it. Freedom for the entire race lay on the other side, they claimed. This is why two divers had been prepared to risk their lives in order to reach it and pass beyond.

The first diver nodded to the second. They hefted the tool and pushed the tip against the barrier. Then they started turning the handle, trying to make the drill bite. But the metal kept slipping.

They stopped work. One of the divers reached out and touched the barrier, feeling it carefully for several minutes.

"What's the matter?" mutely signalled the other.

The first diver made frantic hand gestures. "It's a screwtop! The scientists got it wrong. It's not a cork after all. It must be cheap plonk. The corkscrew is useless. We're stuck in here forever!"

They began the long swim back to the bottom of the bottle.

Twentieth Century Chronoshock

The condition of being allergic to the 20th Century was always going to cure itself in time, but certain members of my profession made matters worse for a minority of victims by meddling with artificial remedies. The truth has only been revealed with the dawn of this new century, the 21st, and the immediate recovery of all who previously suffered the disadvantages of the malady. Because these patients no longer exist in the 20th Century, there is no longer anything in their environment to provoke an allergic reaction. They can be released from quarantine without danger. And so the sealed castles, with their banqueting halls, lutes, jesters and jousting contests can finally be closed down and sold off to private bidders.

However, there remains the problem of what to do with those unlucky individuals who allowed themselves to be experimented upon *prior* to the turn of the century. These patients were promised wonder drugs and surgical miracles to reduce the number of years to which they were sensitive. The first procedures involved cutting out decades from the memory by entering the brain and vandalising it with electric tongs. This technique was only effective at removing the 1980s, which few people cared to remember anyway. Hallucinogenic drugs were also tried, in a bid to erase the 1960s. The problem was that sufferers born after that decade, with no personal experience of it, now no longer remembered they had never been there. They assumed they no longer remembered it because they *had* been there, according to the unique ontological laws governing that decade. Thus their awareness of the 20th Century was extended rather than reduced.

As for removing years from the 20th Century which had occurred before the birth of the patient: there were no memories to extract. With the failure of surgery, it was decided to turn to philosophy. Doubts were raised in the minds of the sufferer as to the concrete reality of a non-experiential year. Reality is unreal, and all things are illusions. A man or woman born in 1935 might thus be persuaded that the years 1900-1934 were figments... I dreamt I was a butterfly... flapping my wings and causing a hurricane in Brazil... but for insurance purposes I am not responsible... This approach was powerful. For most of these patients the years of the 20th Century to which they were allergic became fewer and fewer. Unfortunately, it is almost impossible to totally eradicate a malady. There will always be one unit which is immune to the remedy. That's how things evolve! If you don't believe me, order a taxi to the nearest library and consult the biology textbooks. But don't expect me to pay the fare. Read my lips: no new taxis!

Let us consider the consequences of these treatments. We may take a single case. We shall call him Thornton E. to disguise the fact his real surname is Excelsior. Don't want to embarrass him! Thornton volunteered for these experiments. The years to which he was allergic fell away rapidly. Soon he was only allergic to a single year: 1957! He was released from quarantine and was able to live in society like a normal citizen, but with a crucial difference: any exposure to the products, situations or ideas of 1957 would bring him out in a monumental rash, a rash almost larger than his body. So, for instance, references to the death of Joseph McCarthy, the launching of Sputnik I, the sacking of Marshal Zhukov from his post as Minister of Defence, the drawing of the first premium bond prize in the UK, the sending of 1000 Army paratroopers to Arkansas to escort nine black students into the Central High School in the town of Little Rock, the unveiling of the Jodrell Bank radio telescope, not to mention several trillion other things, would instantly propel Thornton E. into a cosmos of rash, for merely to state that he would "come out in one" is to fail at producing the right effect with words.

It might not seem difficult to avoid the trappings of 1957 or any other single year of the previous century. On first appearance, this condition may appear preferable to being allergic to the entire century. But consider more carefully and you will appreciate the irony. The untreated patients, those who remained allergic to the entire century, discovered that their ailment completely disappeared on the stroke of midnight on New Year's Eve 1999 (ending the debate about the true beginning of the next millennium). Nothing in their environment was now part of the 20th Century, because the past only exists as memories, recorded or not, and the present is all we have. They became totally free. However, the treated patients remained allergic to the details of their most stubborn years, whether that year was 1957, as in the case of Thornton E., or 1914, 1938, 1976, 1991, etc.

I have found a neat use for these unfortunates. I have gathered together one hundred of them. Each is allergic to a different year from 1900-1999 so that the complete century is covered. I drive them around in a bus. I have changed careers. I now assist collectors and detectives with their hobbies and investigations. If an antiques-dealer wants to know the date of a piece of merchandise, to establish whether it is genuine, he summons me. If a forensic pathologist is unsure of how long a skeleton has been hanging in a closet, he rings my office without delay. I drive the bus to the relevant scene. The hundred men and women in my care are numbered. I usher them in single-file past the ornament or cadaver. The one who comes out in a rash reveals the date! If there is no rash, then the merchandise or crime is very recent or quite old. I still accept payment. In the evenings I relax by playing hop frog with the leap-years.

The Psychoanalyst

Zimmer knocked on the door and waited for Brando to grunt, "Enter!" then he turned the handle and stepped smartly into the office. A thin room, poky, without windows, cluttered with all manner of oddments, few of them work-related.

Brando didn't glance up, "What may I do for you?"

Zimmer cleared his throat.

Brando stopped stroking the keys of his computer, turned slowly to fix his pale eyes on the intruder. "Well?"

"They say you're a psychoanalyst," said Zimmer.

Brando smiled. "That's true."

"I need help," hissed Zimmer. "Can you help me?"

Brando sighed, shrugged his shoulders at his computer, gestured at the documents on his desk. "I'm busy."

Zimmer moistened his dry lips with his tongue. "I'm sorry for coming here unannounced, without making an appointment. I was upstairs and overheard some marketing people talking about you. They said you were a psychoanalyst, so I lost no time seeking you out. I'm on my break."

"This is rather unorthodox," muttered Brando.

Zimmer pouted. "I hope you might spare just five minutes of your time. You see, I have a problem, an issue that's bothering me, and it won't leave me alone. I need to talk about it to a professional. Please say you'll listen! I'll pay double your fee!"

Brando held up a hand. "Money's not important."

Zimmer looked around the room for a couch, but there wasn't even a spare chair, so he remained standing, closed his eyes and spoke quickly, as if he feared Brando would lose interest before he reached the end. "It's about death, life after death. And it's about time, the compression of time. About individual experiences and how they can alter the perception of passing time, so it seems to flow at different speeds for people who are under dissimilar circumstances. About how time can flow at several different speeds at the same time!"

"Life after death," echoed Brando quietly.

"It recently occurred to me," continued Zimmer, "that for people who are dying, the subjective experience of time might slow down to the point where it stops in relation to an outside observer. We all know that in situations of extreme peril, a period of time as short as one tenth of a second may be subjectively extended until it feels like minutes. As peril increases, the expansion of time also increases. What if there's no limit to this process? What if the onrush of death is such an extreme event that it makes subjective time stretch to infinity?"

Brando examined his fingernails. "In that case, the dying person would become immortal, at least from their own perspective. From an external perspective, they would continue to die until they were dead. So eternal life after death and oblivion would both occur simultaneously. It's an interesting concept and not illogical. After all, it's perfectly possible for an infinite series of tasks or steps to take place in a finite time. In fact it happens every moment. There are an infinite number of fractions of time between one second and the next, but that second still passes. So you have devised a new theory of eschatology, the study of life after death. Well done! But none of this has anything to do with me."

Zimmer trembled. "Yes it does! The ramifications are profoundly disturbing! I can't get out of my mind the thought that everybody who has ever died is possibly still alive inside his or her own subjective time frame! The idea is overwhelming, debilitating, and it obsesses me night and day. I need to expel it from my system. Can you help?"

Brando frowned and stroked his chin. "Not really. That's not my line of work. If you had come to me with streams of numerical figures I could have put them into graph form for you, but when it comes to crises of the soul, I'm as ignorant as the next man."

Zimmer blinked. "But you're a psychoanalyst! You admitted it. If you can't help me, then who can?"

"Well, maybe I *can* help you. We could do an experiment. But tell me first: does anyone else know you're here?"

Zimmer shook his head. "I came down on impulse. I didn't tell any of my colleagues. I'm willing to try anything!"

Brando nodded. "Good." He stood and opened a metal box standing on a shelf. Then he rummaged inside and extracted a glittering curved knife and a roll of duct tape. He cut a length of tape and closed the box, then approached Zimmer with a wink.

Zimmer laughed uneasily. "What are you doing?"

Brando pounced before Zimmer could turn, pushing him onto the floor and forcing the tape over his mouth. He didn't bother locking the door. Nobody ever came to see him anyway.

He moved his mouth close to Zimmer's ear. "Yes, I'm an analyst. A data analyst. I just happen to be a psycho as well. A psychopath. That's why they call me a *psycho analyst*. I'm a data analyst who's a psycho, but I do my job well, so they keep me on."

He bound Zimmer's hands and legs together and started work with his curved blade. He was a craftsman, a specialist. An hour later, he paused and spoke to the place where an ear had been.

"Has time stopped yet? Has it stopped?"

The Blanket Ban

I wanted to impose a blanket ban on all blanket bans; but would I be able to do so before the ban came into force? I doubted it. After all, I'm incapable of travelling faster than logic, not even when mounted on my smoothest castors. The people asked me in chattering dismay:

"Why do you wish to ban blankets at this time of year?"

"I don't intend to ban blankets," I explained patiently, "but to ban bans."

They refused to listen. "It's very cold."

"Ban bans," I repeated.

"Winter seems endless. Even our fires have frozen, each tongue of flame turning into an icicle, a hot icicle true enough, but still an icicle."

"Ban, ban, you're dead." I was exasperated.

97

The truth is that I hate being absolute ruler of this planet. Don't misinterpret my wish; I have no desire to be an underling. No, I would like to be an overling, if there is such a thing. Or maybe just a ling.

I wish I had the power but not the worry.

Ding dong, said my doorbell.

This was surprising. I wasn't expecting any visitors. "Come in, the bolts are drawn back!" I shouted, but I loosened my duelling dagger in its sheath. A familiar face appeared: it belonged to you, the reader.

"No more stories about cold weather, please!" you said.

"That's not up to me..." I objected.

"You might at least *try* to do something about the situation."

"Sure." What else could I say?

I went for a walk outside. Two men were fencing with fire icicles in one of the courtyards, not because they hated each other but as a cheap way to stay warm. I left the palace and undulated myself over the deserted dunes towards the sea. The vast expanse of water was grey, a reflection of the clouds above. I say 'clouds' but really I mean just one single unbroken *cloud*, a mass of vaporous greyness that had been stuck in place for months. I sighed.

My breath was the exhaust of a rocket engine, but as rockets hadn't yet been invented it must have been more like something else instead, the steam of a boiling tea kettle or the smoke of a tiny volcano.

Could it be that the world was sleeping? That it had overslept?

If this was true, then the cloud would be the blanket of an enormous bed and the land and sea —

geography itself in fact — would be snuggled under it, reluctant to get up, disinclined to face a chilly day.

"Wakey, wakey, rise and shine!" I shouted.

But that wasn't strong enough.

It was the blanket that was preventing the sleeper being warmed by the sun, and the cold sleeper was determined not to cast off the blanket that it thought was keeping it warmer than it would otherwise be. This loop of irony had to be broken somewhere; and suddenly I knew how...

The aroma of coffee. That was the only answer!

Coffee is a smell that can entice even the most sluggish sleeper out of bed, a beguiling odour that crooks like a beckoning finger and uses the hook of that crook to yank the somnambulant snorer upright. The blankets are pushed away and slide off the bed of their own accord and so...

Another new day! The world needed a new day.

I returned to the palace and summoned messengers. I used other messengers to summon them. After they arrived I instructed them and sent them away to all the lands where coffee beans can be obtained.

Within a few days, the beans began arriving in wagons, carts, trucks, barrels, baskets and satchels. I ordered them crushed into dust under the feet of hephalumps and the powder conveyed to the sea and dumped. Waves churned it. Time went on and matters continued in this exact fashion.

Eventually the ocean was salt water no longer, but coffee.

Yet it was *cold* coffee, still no good.

It didn't smell enticing; it smelled unpleasant, gelid, bitter.

There had to be a way of heating it up.

Fortunately at that moment, an undersea volcano decided to erupt. Maybe it had been inspired by the exhalation of my breath fifteen paragraphs previously? Or maybe it had some other reason to blow its top?

Who can divine the ways of seismic disturbance? Not I.

The coffee boiled, the aroma wafted into the sky; and then, to the astounding glee of everyone below, the endless solitary cloud peeled back. One corner simply receded upwards and it dragged the rest along.

Geography had woken up at last!

I ordered croissants, *lots* of them, to be scattered in strategic locations across the realm. Then I adjusted my crown sententiously. I had failed to ban blanket bans but had succeeded in banning blankets instead.

The sun sparkled on my castors.

Read this story in the morning for maximum benefit.

Kharms Before the Storm
(A story in the style of Daniil Kharms)

Kharms said to Lakoba, "Do you mind if I ask you a question?"

Lakoba answered, "No, go ahead."

Kharms remained silent.

Lakoba gasped, "Well? Go on, I'm waiting!"

100

Kharms frowned. "Waiting for what?"

Lakoba cried, "For the question!"

Kharms replied, "But I asked it and you gave me your answer. I asked, do you mind if I ask you a question? *That* was my question. And you answered: no, go ahead."

Lakoba reddened. "In that case you asked your question before I gave you my permission to ask it."

Kharms said, "Does that make you angry?"

Lakoba bellowed, "Livid!"

Kharms shrugged. "Nonetheless I am satisfied."

Without hesitation, Lakoba rushed at Kharms, twisted his arms behind his back and threw him out the window.

NOTE: Daniil Kharms (1905-1942) was born in St Petersburg; after criticism from the Soviet authorities his writings were suppressed and he found himself unable to publish anything, yet he continued writing. He specialised in absurd and rather monstrous flash fictions that often featured people falling out of windows. Imprisoned, he was deliberately starved to death.

Keep Kharms and be an Absurdist
(Another story in the style of Daniil Kharms)

Ivan Oknov was a man with red hair and one black tooth. He bumped into another man on the corner of Askance Street. The other man had black hair and one red tooth and his name was Navi Vonko.

You bumped into me, Navi said.

No, you bumped into me, responded Ivan.

I think it was you into me.

101

On the contrary, it was you into me.

But I was already bumped into, by you, when I bumped into you, Navi argued and his tone was so fierce that it became entirely reasonable to believe his version of events. So Ivan said:

Very well, have it your way. But what's the rush anyway?

I'm rushing to work, that's where, said Navi.

Me too, said Ivan. To work.

I make money doing what I love to do, declared Navi.

What might that be? asked Ivan.

Advising people on how to make money doing what they love to do, came the reply. That's what I love to do and I get paid for doing it. I get paid in money, real money, for that. What do you do?

I do what I don't love doing. I wring the necks of clocks.

Wring the necks of clocks, you said?

I said that, exactly that.

Well, I can show you how to make money doing what you love to do instead. I can show you in ten minutes.

I wouldn't like that, said Ivan uneasily.

Why not? Why not? Navi cried.

Because I love to lose money, that's what I love to do; and if I made money doing that, if I made money losing it, then I would never lose any, and I wouldn't be doing what I love doing, which is losing money, so how could I make money doing what I love? It's impossible.

Navi considered this carefully. A truck was approaching down the road. Suddenly he grabbed hold of Ivan and threw himself into the path of the vehicle and they were both crushed to death.

Doom Laden Haven

This is the way the world ends.

In fact it was scheduled to end in many different ways. There was disagreement among scientists about which catastrophe was most likely. Bets were made.

"A deadly new virus will kill all life."

"No, a comet will strike the Earth first."

"Not a comet: an asteroid!"

"Rubbish. A giant volcano will erupt somewhere and cover everything with lava and hot ash."

"Tidal waves will destroy us before that!"

The planet Earth is the safest place in the solar system but it is still doom laden. That's the way these scientists liked it. Without the threat of global annihilation they would be out of a job.

How would they feel if the world was never destroyed? Disgruntled in the extreme. In fact some of them had made a secret pact: if the world suddenly didn't look like it was ever going to end, if evidence emerged that it was stable and secure, they would take matters into their own hands.

The scientists were furious when all their predictions came true at the same time — and cancelled each other out!

A comet landed in the sea and caused a tidal wave that washed over a giant volcano that had just erupted. The wave extinguished the volcano and the violent jet of steam created from the meeting of water and fire spurted high into the atmosphere and slowed the descent of an onrushing asteroid, lowering it gently to the ground where it plugged the volcano. A deadly new virus that was about to ravage populations was cured by another virus carried on the comet that was dispersed in the sea. The two viruses turned on each other until both were extinct.

True to their word, the scientists who had made the secret pact tricked their way into missile bases and launched a nuclear attack on all cities. Some of them had security clearance. Mushroom clouds sprouted everywhere. A risotto of death.

"This place looks just like Eden! And my name is Eve, really it is! And we are the last two people left on Earth, probably. The *last* couple! There must be some reason for all this. What is your name?"

The man covered his nakedness with a fig leaf.

"My name?" he mumbled.

"Yes, your name! I told you mine, I am called Eve. A significant name, don't you think? Eve!"

"I suppose so," he agreed.

"What is *your* name?" she pressed.

Finally he remembered. "Twitterhouse Gumplung," he said.

Her face fell with disappointment.

The Metaphorical Marriage

She was as open as turquoise, as smug as a crouton, as whipped as a hat, as judicious as bronze, as broken as an indoor wasp. She lived in a dark house like a foot in a bracket, like a god in a hog, like a departure in the afternoon.

She was married to a man with eyebrows as damp as cheese, with morals as pale as clues, with pity as deep as paprika. They had not kissed for a saddle of years. They simply ignored each other: like teeth on holiday, like lakes in a book, like an ounce and a pound, like a sock and a poem.

They had different interests and separate appetites, as if a pair of assassins had divorced their poisons and shaved the manners from their daggers. Their lives were like kidneys.

One day, the woman grew a lover. So the man was forced to recognise her in the asthmatic corridor.

"You've changed," he said. "You look like a trumpet in the dawn, a noodle in a shire, a crotchet in sauce."

With a nod, she replied, "The creative writing class is making you ill. Matthew is a journalist. He will film your decay."

The husband saw that the lover had a tripod and lens, both as sleek as sugar and practical as floss. He did not want to comply, but had little choice.

Matthew followed his language over the house, calling, "Simile, you're on candied camera!"

The husband was trapped in a loveless metaphor.

The Casual Comment

A shirt once said to a jacket, "The button on the end of my sleeve seems to be on the verge of coming loose."

"What do you expect me to do about it?" asked the jacket.

"Nothing I suppose," said the shirt.

"Don't bother me with trifles, I'm busy," said the jacket.

"With trifles? There are no trifles in here. This is a wardrobe, not a pantry. You are very confused."

"The child who lives in this house often hides trifles and other desserts in this wardrobe," cried the jacket defensively.

"Fair enough, but trifles have nothing to do with me. I was telling you about the button on my sleeve."

"I don't want to hear about it!" roared the jacket.

Suddenly the button fell off.

As it fell and clattered to the bottom of the wardrobe it shouted, "This is great fun! I'm flying just like a phoenix but without the wings or the beak or the legends or the immortality."

"That's a very off-the-cuff remark," said the jacket.

The shirt creased with laughter...

Flash in the Pantheon

We all loved the maestro. But he deserved to die. He tapped his baton on the music stand and the orchestra finished tuning up and settled down. A hush fell over the audience. A large black cloud on collision course with another checked its flight. The air was a-shimmer with expectancy. Hands froze on their popcorn; no one breathed. Fans were held rigid and smiles were fixed. Bosoms were still.

Suddenly, with a mighty sweep and a flick of his unkempt hair, he loosed himself upon the world.

The orchestra exploded into action. The clouds collided like dark cymbals. The air vibrated with raw energy. Hands shovelled popcorn into mouths; everyone gasped. Fans waved wildly and smiles grew bigger. Bosoms heaved.

High above that enraptured crowd, I saw how the sky was beginning to change. The clouds had settled their differences and had joined forces. More of their fellows clambered over the horizon to greet them. All other eyes were on the maestro's baton. It gouged trenches in the fabric of reality. Faster and faster and faster.

As its velocity increased, the audience began to mutter to themselves. They had never seen anything quite like this before. Not even at the outdoor concert hosted by the great Alberti. So they shook their heads and rolled their eyes in admiration. Finally they could contain themselves no longer and cried out:

"He's moving too quickly!"

"The orchestra is struggling to keep up!"

I smiled indulgently at their excitement. But there was a curious doubt at the back of my mind. I attempted to express it through a frown. It had seemed absurd to hold such a concert at this time of the year. The outdoor program should not have started for at least another month. But the maestro had always been eager to take risks. The weathermen had pleaded with him to delay; they could not promise clemency. In return he had merely laughed at them and thumbed his nose at the brooding sky.

His baton was now a blur of speed. The musicians grew red in the face. The brass section keeled over as one. The strings of cellos and violas snapped or burst into flame. Yet still he urged them onwards. A single droplet of sweat hung from the tip of his nose. The audience hugged themselves and mumbled platitudes ripe with astonishment:

"He has left the orchestra behind!"

"Such speed is positively preternatural!"

And at once I realised what the doubt in the back of my mind was trying to say. I consulted the expanding clouds and understood that they too shared my concern. A terrible itch spread along my fingers and up my hand. I shifted uneasily in my chair.

Faster and faster raced the maestro. The sonic boom would not be long coming. The clouds trembled and knocked together. The musicians themselves began to ignite. The audience rose to its feet to cheer, but a surge of power crushed all back into their seats. The maestro was oblivious to all this; his head was down, his pose as arrogant as ever. At last the clouds cried out for justice and I had to oblige.

I reached into my pocket for a bolt, twirled it between finger and thumb and hurled it down. It struck the maestro on the head and instantly reduced him to a pile of ashes.

There was a single outburst: "Bravo!"

I felt guilty, of course, but consoled myself with a deep musical sigh. There was nothing I could do. It was to be expected, after all. It was his own fault. And when the audience gazed upwards to ask why, I had this answer for them:

"He was a lightning conductor."

The Moon and the Well

Once again, the moon is setting behind the old well at the bottom of the garden. Our slack faces crowd at the window, noses pressed to frosty glass, eyeing the falling moon. Lower and lower it sinks until it has completely vanished. Once a month we wait for this moment, we ache in the silence. At other times, rocking on our wormy chairs, rubbing our bony knees in front of a dying fire, we seek to fill space with songs and timid stories. But no words can emerge from our drooling mouths. We need the laughter of a child, the warmth of youth. We listen for the sound, the splash of water that will redeem us.

Together, trembling hand in hand, we race down the garden path, dragging our nets behind us. We have not been deceived. Our long wait is over. The moon has missed the horizon and fallen into the well. We pull up the gurgling moon in a bucket and plunge our nets into the depths. The moon struggles beneath the silver liquid, a ladder of moonbeams rippling on the waves of emotion that sweep over us. It is a very new moon. From now on, the nights will always be dark. In the corner of a ruined cottage we will set up a cot. Through the bars of this cot we will feed our lunar child with a long-handled spoon.

Christmas Overtime

It is Christmas again, of course it is, and a full stop has been placed quite deliberately, like a glacé cherry, at the end of the year. This time, though, you are excluded from the festivities. You have lost the chance to eat, drink and make Mary. Christmas is red rotund, noble and inane, but you are not. You cannot spill the cream of indulgence down the shirtfront of success. You cannot laugh when neighbours toast your health with your own Malt. You cannot choke on the wishbone of convention.

So now you decide to cut through the season with a serrated truth. You decide to fight back. There is no goodwill to all men, at least none without an ulterior motive, and you will tear away this canvas of delusion and expose the facts as they are, a process as painful as the breaking of a tooth on a sixpence concealed in a pudding.

But how can you do it? Is there anything you can do? You ponder this over. Yes, there is one thing. There is one balloon you can burst before its time, one cracker you can defuse, one fairy light you can ground to coloured glass.

His door is ajar. You peer through the crack. His eyes are open. They are large, moist, round. You almost falter before taking the fateful step, but then, sudden intoxicating courage overwhelming, you push forward.

You enter without knocking. He turns towards you and smiles. There is unaffected joy in his smile. There is excitement intolerable. His stocking hangs large and empty. The tree in the corner winks its tiny lights. You are not what he is waiting for, but it is early yet. The hands of the clock pass very slowly.

Good evening, you say, and the awkward pause threatens to drown your resolution, drown it in his large, moist, round eyes. But you are still drunk with purpose. So with a breath as deep as a snowdrift, you continue.

There is no Father Christmas, you announce, savouring the effect of these negative words. There is no Father Christmas and no reindeer sleigh. There is no such bulky benefactor, and thus no hand in a fur-trimmed glove to fill your stocking.

And, of course, he bursts into tears. You are a liar, he wails, and yet as he voices these words, he knows in his heart that you are right and that his dreams are gossamer webs, baubles to be trampled underfoot, pine needles to be shaken loose and swept away.

And triumphant, you close the door and return to your desk, while the sobs of your boss echo through the deserted office.

The Googol Seasons

As they filed into the church, the music students lowered their voices and smoothed their paisley. They took to their seats and waited for the corners of the hush to fill the nave.

Stragglers stumbled over the legs of others. A few sickly souls grasped the opportunity to vent a cough.

The orchestra tuned up and, with a flick of fringe, the great virtuoso himself, Solomon Bowe, made his entrance.

There was an excited murmuring from the audience.

"How handsome he is!"

"What a superb fringe!"

"What an exquisite violin!"

"Who can play Vivaldi like Solomon Bowe?"

"No one!"

Without further ado, the master struck up the opening to *The Four Seasons,* that perennial favourite. Since graduating with honours from the Lycée d'Faust, Solomon had refused to play anything else. Vivaldi exerted a strange hold over him.

The seasons rolled like flavours on the tongue. Spring, summer, the darker moods of autumn and winter. With the final chord echoing in their ears, the students burst into applause.

Undaunted, Solomon began the first movement again.

"What's going on? This isn't supposed to happen!"

From the rear of the church came a desperate shout: "The doors are locked. There's no way out."

And then, as slowly as roots pushing through frosty soil, the truth dawned. The passage of the real seasons is circular, they have no end. The playing of a single year was not enough for Solomon Bowe. Not enough by a long geological chalk deposit.

He was going for the aeon...

Funny Bone

Fiona fell and fractured her funny bone. It was no joke. She couldn't laugh at anything now, no matter how hilarious it might be. Farces, slapstick, puns and all other kinds of comedy left her cold. She just sat there with a forced smile on her lips. Her sense of humour didn't work.

She waited for her funny bone to heal, to knit together, but the doctors told her it was a forlorn hope. "That won't happen by itself and there's no way we can put a splint on it. A funny bone isn't a real bone, that's why, but simply a psychological inclination. We can't fix those."

To forget her troubles Fiona went on holiday

and got extremely drunk in the capital city of France. A few days after the inevitable hangover she found herself laughing at something and then she realised she was better after all. So she returned home to baffle her doctors.

Only she would ever understand the reason for the cure. Her funny bone was set accidentally due to the special circumstances of her drunken exploit. She had got plastered in Paris.

The Knees

It was so foggy that Boris Martins could only see his own knees ahead of him on the road. The headlights of the parked car cut through the thick white soup of the fog and illuminated his knees, and only those, because they were on the same level, the knees and the headlights. So they were the only things he was able to discern.

He frowned down at them because they didn't look quite right. The knee on the left looked a bit like a ghost. The knee on the right looked a bit like a psycho. This made him scared. As if aware that he was scared and wishing to scare him even more, the knees began knocking together like the horrid drums of a voodoo ritual.

"What do you want?" Leave me alone!" he screamed at them.

"Noooooo!" wailed the right knee.

"I want to kill you!" cackled the left knee.

The headlights went out. The battery had died. Boris Martins was on his own. His soul had never felt so cold. Then he felt something crawling up his thigh, two things, one on each thigh. Higher and higher they went, up his pelvis, up his stomach and chest. Finally they reached his throat, a pair of ghastly disconnected hungry knees!

Boris Martins never kneeled again in church or elsewhere.

N+ Prime

N+0

There was no jam in the pot. I turned to my wife and cried, "If I can't have jam, I won't have toast. Bring me honey on biscuits instead!" But my wife lost her temper and hit me over the head with a heavy dictionary. Then everything, time and space included, went funny.

N+1

There was no Japanese in the potato. I turned to my wildlife and cried, "If I can't have Japanese, I won't have tobacco. Bring me honour on bishops instead!" But my wildlife lost her temperature and hit me over the headache with a heavy diesel. Then everything, timetable and speaker included, went funny.

N+2

There was no jar in the potential. I turned to my willingness and cried, "If I can't have jar, I won't have toe. Bring me hook on bits instead!" But my willingness lost her temple and hit me over the heading with a heavy diet. Then everything, timing and specialist included, went funny.

N+3

There was no jaw in the pound. I turned to my wind and cried, "If I can't have jaw, I won't have toilet. Bring me hope on bladders instead!" But my wind lost her temptation and hit me over the headline with a heavy difference. Then everything, tin and species included, went funny.

N+5

There was no jean in the powder. I turned to my wine and cried, "If I can't have jeans, I won't have ton. Bring me horn on blankets instead!" But my wine lost her tendency and hit me over the headquarters with a heavy dignity. Then everything, tissue and specimen included, went funny.

N+7

There was no Jew in the practice. I turned to my winner and cried, "If I can't have Jew, I won't have tongue. Bring me horse on blocks instead!" But my winner lost her tension and hit me over the heap with a heavy dimension. Then everything, toast and spectator included, went funny.

N+11

There was no joke in the precedent. I turned to my wish and cried, "If I can't have joke, I won't have top. Bring me hostility on blues instead!" But my wish lost her terrace and hit me over the heating with a heavy direction. Then everything, tomato and speed included, went funny.

Note+0: The technique known as "N+0" can be applied to any text: simply substitute each noun with the noun zero places after it in any dictionary. The transformed text often makes more sense than the original!

Note+1: The technology known as "N+1" can be applied to any textile: simply suburb each noun with the noun one placement after it in any diesel. The transformed textile often makes more sensitivity than the original!

Note+2: The telegraph known as "N+2" can be applied to any theft: simply successor each noun with the noun two plants after it in any difficulty. The transformed theft often makes more sentiment than the original!

Note+3: The temper known as "N+3" can be applied to any theory: simply suggestion each noun with the noun three plates after it in any dining. The transformed theory often makes more serum than the original!

Note+5: Etc.

The Snail Path

Every day glittered with the futility of his labour in the ball-bearing factory. Every night, several pints only increased his inward emptiness. When he reached home and looked at the sky, the unavoidable stars sparkled like a thousand million baleful ball bearings littered through the darkness of spacetime. The snails were his salvation. Every night, they were there when he looked down. A host in slow and slimy procession across the drive. Why? He would never understand. Why did they leave a bed of comfortable and tasty salad vegetables and cross the barren tarmac only to reach an unfriendly grass border by the wall the other side?

This solemn, creepy journey could not be for nothing. They knew what they were about. Earth-centered, they had purpose. He contemplated with envy the nature of snails. His speech slurred, his instinct to hide grew stronger; he developed a penchant for lettuce, a horror of salt. One day, he took up the challenge of the last ball bearing. He gave in his notice. His wife found him on the drive covered in slime, his body hunched inside the linen basket, curtain wires hooked around his ears quivering as antennae. His eyes were tight shut. He knew what he was about. He had taken the snail path.

The Business Diary of a Madman

Monday, May 11
Meet Harrison for lunch.

Tuesday, May 12
Finish report on Saudi deal.
Lunch with Schulz.
Call Orton about shipment of faulty solenoids.

Wednesday, May 13
Health & Safety Inspectors. Be polite!
Buffet at Yacht Club.
Minnear due for flea in ear.

Thursday, May 14
Interview graduates for temporary technician post.
Schulz says Bingham most likely not to pick nose.
Auditors here, keep cool.
Sinclair's funeral, collect suit from cleaners.
Salads with Harrison.

Delegation from Paris, broach champagne. If enthusiastic, show them the R&D lab. Keep them away from O'Casey.

Dressing down for Collins.

Friday, May 15
Seminar at institute.

Lunch with Orton and Jagger. Discuss terms of new contract.

Promotion for Schulz.

Ring Singapore branch, recall Clarke. Tell him to take economy class and resist duty free. If he refuses, threaten to make public his affair with Hawkins. Reverse charges of call.

Dismiss Babbage.

Dinner with Jessica. Avoid references to electrocution.

Saturday, May 16
Open and read birthday cards!

Try on new shirt.

Quick round of golf with Harrison.

Supermarket: two lemons, whole chicken, organic potatoes, mushrooms, eggs and flour, parsnips, olive oil.

Return library books, pay fine.

Stroll to hardware store: spade, claw hammer.

Back in time for Auntie Mabel.

Ring Jessica, blow her one kiss only. No voltages jokes.

Dark clothes for cemetery.

Sunday, May 17
Wash car.

Cut grass and trim hedge.

Write letter to Auntie Mabel thanking her for the wonderful black jumper she gave me for my birthday. Very useful.

Clean spade, dispose of nails.

Sunday dinner with Sinclair.

The Locksmith

High in the trees he was, as usual, when the visitor came. He swung down, branch to branch until he was dangling only half the length of a long banana from the parched ground. The visitor had four, five, six times as many wrinkles over his entire body as he, the host, had years of life. Thus does a rhinoceros compare with a bonobo ape.

"Good morning. Welcome to my humble abode."

It was a good idea to get the formalities out of the way before starting work. *Why* there had to be any formalities was a question that no one seemed prepared to ask. It was just a case of common courtesy, of continuing a tradition that might be important in some hidden way; perhaps also to intensify the general ironic effect.

"Thank you," said the rhinoceros.

"Have you travelled far? Are you in good health? Please make yourself at home. What can I do for you?"

But there was only one thing he could ever do for any of his numerous visitors: the question had been asked for its rhythm rather than its sense. The rhino didn't need to reply. Animals came to Obo the Bonobo for a single specific reason; and everybody knew it. The rhino waited while the ape examined the collar locked around his neck.

"It's a standard model," Obo said.

"Not too big a job for you?"

Obo shook his head and climbed back up the tree, almost to the very top, where he called down, "Not at all. Easy. They haven't changed this style for three years, but I suppose they will soon. The designers they use aren't very imaginative and therefore—"

The rustling of leaves in a sudden gust made the ending of the sentence unintelligible to the rhino, who continued to wait.

Obo climbed down, an iron object in his mouth.

"Is that the right key?" the rhino asked.

"Mmmmfph," came the answer; then Obo reached the ground again and removed it from his mouth. "Yes, it is."

"I knew it would be," said the rhino.

"Even if I didn't have a suitable key, I could pick the lock without any trouble; and in the unlikely event of a new design withstanding my abilities, I would simply cut the collar off."

"Is that a split infinitive?" wondered the rhino.

Obo frowned. "What?"

"You said 'cut the collar off' instead of 'cut off the collar'. I don't know if that's an example of a split infinitive or not. To be honest, I couldn't care less. I'm grateful anyway."

"Good," said Obo. He reached up and inserted the key.

"That tickles," giggled the rhino.

"Does it really?" Obo gave the key a sharp turn.

"No," admitted the rhino.

The collar fell to the ground with a metallic clang. Obo bent over it and nodded to himself. Then he went to fetch a hammer and chisel and carefully removed the radio tracking device, leaving the remainder of the heavy collar in the dust. He threw back his head and whooped at the sky, and a tiny dot extremely high above began a steady descent.

"A vulture," explained Obo.

"Ah, very clever!"

"Anything to generate maximum confusion."

"You are ingenious."

"So I've been told." Obo sighed happily.

The vulture landed, scuffed up a cloud of yellow dust, waited for Obo to approach with the transmitter clutched in one hand. Then the beak opened and closed on the device and great wings flapped ponderously; the enormous bird took off and flew away over the trees. Obo went into some bushes and rummaged among the leaves.

He emerged carrying another transmitter. "This is for you."

"I understand. My part of the bargain."

"We must all help each other," said Obo.

"Whom did it belong to?"

"Believe it or not, a dolphin. The coast is only twenty miles that way. I go there every so often." The ape pointed to the east. The rhino accepted the device by lowering his head: it was lashed to a loop of vine and slid comfortably over his horn.

"This is very funny. I intend to head inland."

"Of course. Maximum confusion!"

"Maximum confusion!" agreed the rhino. "Thank you."

"Please don't mention it."

"But I already did. Farewell." He trotted off.

Obo waited until he was out of sight then he inserted his arm into a crack in a toppled tree and pulled out a scroll. He unrolled it on the ground and held it flat with small stones; with the tip of a charred stick he updated his accounts. It was important to keep track of each and every new deception. Then he carefully replaced the scroll.

Climbing back up into the jungle canopy he waited for his second visitor of the day, the next tagged animal. He wondered how the different teams of researchers would interpret the results.

Feeling he was making real progress, he peeled a banana.

On the Deck

After dinner, they went out on deck.

"Money is the root of all revel," said Laura, as she sipped the last of the champagne and tossed her glass casually over the side. "Don't you think so?"

"Absolutely." Jerry felt sick. He grasped the rails and bent his head forward. The Beef Chasseur in his stomach began to churn.

"And how delicious the moon is!" Laura added, leaning back and pouting, her fingers idly worrying the beads that looped around her swan's neck. "Big and round."

"Enormous." Jerry clutched his sides and gasped. His cravat had come askew, his cufflinks glittered in the 'delicious' light. He was enjoying himself but little.

"And the swell of the sea, the splash of the

fish..."

"Extraordinary."

Laura sighed and lit a cigarette. There were, in fact, no fish to speak of, nor swell of the sea. But there *was* a moon, so massive and heavy that the proverbial lunar man must surely have filled his cheeks with apples...

Jerry turned his sallow face towards Laura and said, in a voice not unlike a croak:

"I will be happy when we reach land."

"Oh, really!" Laura was exasperated. She inhaled her cigarette in languid disappointment, the curl of the blue smoke rising up to kiss her kiss-curl. "Sometimes I think that you don't really enjoy travelling."

"It's not that," Jerry protested. "It's just that I can't shake off the feeling that something is not quite right. I mean, where are all the other passengers? And why does the Captain keep changing our destination?"

"He's a wonderful man," Laura replied. "All this was his idea. I never thought I would travel. Especially not in such style. We owe him a lot."

Jerry expressed doubt.

"He winked at me tonight," Laura said, realising it for the first time, according it exaggerated significance as a result, and trying to repress a hot flush and a giggle. "He might even touch my knee tomorrow."

"Bah!" Although Jerry was jealous, he did not feel left out. He too had an amorous secret. The Captain had also winked at him...

"I think we're heading for Ceylon," Laura said, "where the girls are lithe and mysterious and their hair smells of sandalwood."

123

"It's Sri Lanka now," Jerry corrected. "Besides, you're thinking of Burma. They wear little bells around their ankles and they capture little birds in cages just to release them again. Rather odd, don't you think? Just a trifle odd?"

"Not at all. I think it's very beautiful. If only I could find a man strong enough to capture me and then let me go again, I would be happy. To be enticed and then rejected out of love..."

"You're such a decadent!" cried Jerry.

Laura smiled a wry smile and adopted a decadent pose. She had read enough French novels to know that true decadence is affected, and that it is the pose that counts. "Alas!" she said, for no good reason.

Music drifted on the still air, a suitably romantic waltz that washed over them, and over the rails, into the night.

"The band!" Laura squeaked. "How perfect! We must dance immediately! Take me in your arms and spin me around, your sensuous mouth fixed on mine!"

"I'd rather not." Jerry turned green at the prospect. "My stomach is not up to it at present. And you've got to maintain a sense of proportion."

"On the contrary! You've got to dream!" And Laura snatched him by the hand and dragged him close, clasping him savagely and whirling him in a tight spiral. Although he struggled mightily to loosen himself from her clutches, he only managed to free one arm, and this flapped like a flag as she spun him faster and faster.

"How exquisite!" she cried, as they crashed against the rails and rebounded. "How gorgeous! My darling, my swallow, my monstrous orchid!"

Eventually, of course, it was all too much. Jerry

124

threw up.

"I'm sorry," he panted, dejectedly. "It was all too much."

"You wretch, you sombre wretch!" Laura was in tears. She pounded her fists against his chest and wailed. "I'm never coming on another trip with you again! I'm going to seek comfort in the arms of the Captain!"

Jerry had collapsed in a pool of nausea. "I refuse to play anymore!" he groaned.

Laura ignored him and left the deck. The Captain was waiting for her in an easy chair. He had seen everything. "Oh Captain!" she hissed. "It's not fair! You've got to dream, haven't you?"

"Indeed." Smiling gently, I tugged at my magnificent beard and stood up. I was feeling in a benevolent mood. I had already cleared away the remnants of the meal and washed the dishes.

"Sometimes it's the only way to cope with life." She fell into my arms and nestled there like a child. "When life seems drab what else is there?"

"What else?" I echoed. "Yes, you have to dream."

"Oh, Captain! You're a sweet darling. My husband doesn't understand me..."

We were interrupted by an angry knock at the door.

"What was it this time?" I asked her.

She gazed up at me with puppy eyes and blushed. "A champagne glass," she said.

I shook my head disapprovingly, but she could see that my fondness for her had not dissipated. I patted her on the head and winked again. "China tomorrow," I said. "And then Japan."

Before answering the door, I doffed my cap,

125

moved over to the gramophone and lifted the needle off the record.

I hoped that the unexpected caller would accept a bribe. I inspected my wallet. Maintaining the dream was proving expensive. I cast doubtful eyes out onto the deck and listened for the swell of the sea, the splash of the fish.

Twenty floors below, the London traffic flowed onwards.

A Rather Depressed Young Man

This story concerns a rather depressed young man, Simon, who takes himself to the edge of a sea cliff and throws himself over.

What he is really trying to achieve is anyone's guess, though the obvious should not be overlooked. He spins through space and loses consciousness; so relaxed is he now that somehow, miraculously, he survives the landing with no more than a dozen plum bruises on his legs and torso.

Simon is not to know this, however, and when he awakes he assumes that he is dead. But he is aware of his surroundings, so he finally decides that he must be a ghost. There is no other explanation. He stands up and brushes himself down and flexes his ghostly muscles. It is necessary, he thinks, for him to adopt his role completely. He will become an evil spirit. He will do his best to harm people.

So he makes his way back towards the nearest village and waits for his first victim. An elderly man with a false leg totters out of the post office, unsteady on a gnarled stick. Simon kicks away the stick and, once the man is on the ground, removes his false leg and proceeds to batter him to death with it.

Next he wanders into Ye Olde Tea Shoppe and forces a dozen stale scones into the maws of the entire cast of the local Amateur Dramatics Society's production of *Blithe Spirit*. They choke slowly, spitting crumbs and turning blue in real deaths as corny as any they have ever acted.

Several outrages later, as he is in the not entirely unwarranted process of forcing the vicar to eat Mrs Burlington's pink poodle, collar, leash and Mrs Burlington included, he is apprehended by a vengeful mob of cribbage players, retired shopkeepers and ex-servicemen (medals all affixed to jackets at the shortest notice) who chase him out of the village and scream indigo murder.

Simon is surprised they can see him, but is not concerned in the least. They hound him towards the very cliff he earlier had leapt off and this time he does not hesitate: he is a ghost and ghosts can fly.

It is a pity that he is now so tense, with anticipation, with triumph.

The Figure of Speech

She had a great figure of speech.
I metaphor a drink and tried to coax a simile.
She said, "I never cheat when I play on words."
I went home alone…

Eyelashes in my Nepenthe

Driving on the fringes of the city with my head in a sling; concrete overpass, crumbling hi-rise, scrub ballpark. Slinging down the cringes of the frippery with a raw bottled spirit. Ringing down the spirited hinges of the gritty with a ginsling.

My head should ache but doesn't. There is music on the worn-out tape deck. Something too technical: *Larks' Tongues in Aspic* or something similar. More frippery, I suspect. There are ages out here with him, tarmac ages, strata of refuse, casting up archaeological surprises from nigh on twenty years ago. Wrappers of extinct chocolate bars.

I raise the bottle to my lips. Each time I wrench it free, there is an explosion within both cranium and glass. Volatile stuff eh? The lights of passing planes, carrying their cargoes of frightened holidaymakers to the troubled Aegean. But it was your idea dear. Well you said that prices had come down so much. They don't kill independent travellers do they? Only tourists, darling. You stand as much chance of being blown to bits in London as you do there. Besides I've always wanted to see the Turquoise Coast, taste it.

This is the way to the high places, the valleys and castles that smoulder outside urban renewal. The road cuts a swath up into this sardonic land. Come let's drink and laugh. And have a good sticky joke at our own expense, fingers licked with precision, lips lingered with picked incisions, pricks fingered with limp indecision, motions unmoved. Let's turn and sway and load the ballast of emotions that will stabilise our passage through our forgotten youth.

I made that passage in another world, sea-washed, surf as sordid as slag, ambitions as dour as the smoker who turns to tea when tobacco is wanting. The escape was an illusion. All escapes are illusions. One door leads into a room with another two doors. And so on. One garden is pruned and fertilised, but the fountains never splash and the houris never have dark eyes. We've all got to go back home some time. Not yet. Next year maybe. Next decade. We don't complain.

We don't complain. Why should we? What is there to complain about? There is only the smog of the city to plug our nostrils, the grease of the kebab paper to flutter around our legs, the dirt to be removed from under fingernails with the tines of a salad fork, the clouds to haze the day, the buses to demand correct change, the drivers of creaking taxis to meter their wit.

This is the way to the high places. Ascending is more dangerous than descending, but going down is more slippery. Her hair was entangled in my fingers. Her eyes were like knives. Her breasts were like olives, nipples like stones. But she had a pimple on her chin. So passion was a rotting fruit and the haggle was a hag.

In summer I am mocked for not wearing shorts. You are permitted to do as you please provided it is what is expected of you. Sleep has clouded your vision. Might as well play chess on your own, with yourself, and lose despite the fact that you tried to cheat after promising to make the best move possible for both sides. Might as well cook an elaborate meal for yourself with a candle. Might as well grapple with words, send them out into the humid day.

Driving on the fringes of the city with my head in a sling: caught on the moonbeam of a dipped headlamp, ensnared in engine envy, dragged behind those less worthy of such a gift than myself. I loathe and despise them, but only while I have no velocity of my own. It will happen. But at least I know already that the freedom is unreal; I do not need to pay tax on my shattered dreams, insure my immature fantasy. I know what lies out there. I know its price.

Better to pass it with a curt wave than invite it in. Heading down the driveway with a fling in my head. Dreading the highway with the down of her bed still stuck to my blood-orange lips. Grinning down the eyelashes of the city with the drown of her bends distilled in my skull. My head shouldn't ache but it does.

Postmodern Picnic

As Gregor Samsa woke one morning from uneasy metafictional dreams, he found himself transformed into a beetle. Not just any beetle but one with an air-cooled engine, in other words the most famous Volkswagen car ever produced.

For only a moment he was bewildered, then he turned his own ignition and trundled out of his driveway and down the cobbled street.

He had decided to make full use of his new automobile status. He went up the hill to the row of little cottages where his friend Franz lived, stopped outside and honked his horn. A curtain was pulled back in a tiny window and a troubled face peered out. "Hey, it's me!" cried Gregor.

The window was thrown up. "But I don't know anyone called Herbie!" said the face.

"I said Gregor, not Herbie! Are you deaf? You probably don't recognise me looking this way but I suppose that really isn't such a surprise. Nonetheless it *is* me."

The man shut the window and a few seconds later he came out of the door and climbed into Gregor without saying another word. Nor did fasten his seatbelt and in his mind he justified this decision by thinking how odd it would be for a passenger to do that when the driver's seat was empty. Gregor revved his engine. They set off and left the city. There was clearly an unspoken agreement they were going on a picnic, though they had no food.

But they couldn't find the picnic spot. Nowhere was a suitable place for a relaxing external meal and as for the precise location Gregor had in mind it just didn't seem to exist anymore, though Franz thought he glimpsed it once through a parting in the mist, far away. And they both grew old in the search and the food they didn't have went rotten and inedible. Finally it seemed that Gregor couldn't go another mile. "One last try!" urged Franz.

But no, it was useless. Gregor had broken down on the verge. At this point a traffic policeman arrived on his motorbike.

He tapped on the passenger window and Franz wound it down. Though Franz was now very old and his hearing bad, it wasn't necessary for the policeman to shout to make himself heard.

"The picnic spot is just a mile up this road. It was prepared especially for you and only you. I am now going to take away the grass and sky."

And Franz died. For the purposes of a proper ending.

Quiet Flows the Don Juan

He was a great lover. He listened to a song, his lips miming the words. One of the most poignant phrases in this heartfelt piece of work was a plea for an unnamed person to "cry me a river." This unnamed person was a lover who had jilted or betrayed the singer in some manner.

Juan considered the mechanics of this. What exactly is a river? How large does it have to be before it is more than a stream or a brook? He did his research and learned that the largest river in the world, the Amazon, is 2976 miles long with a drainage of 219,000 cubic metres per second, while the smallest is the Roe in Montana, 201 feet in length with a drainage of 156,000,000 gallons per day. A gallon is 4.546 litres and a litre is one cubic decimetre, so he did the conversions and calculations on a piece of paper and worked out that the Amazon is seventy-eight thousand times as long as the Roe and discharges two hundred and seventy times as much water every single second.

So clearly a "river" was a fairly vague concept. To be on the safe side, he took the average of these two extremes and considered the hypothetical result to be the archetypal river of the song. Juan's river was 1489 miles long and drained 109,000 cubic metres of water per second.

How was it possible for a human being to cry such an amount of liquid? A human being is approximately 60% water, so that a man weighing 70 kilograms will contain about 40 litres, or twenty seven thousand times less than the amount drained by Juan's river every second. In order to cry a river, a human eye would have to be scaled up until it was

685 metres in diameter. A person with such a massive eye would obviously have to be a giant and, thanks to gravity, unable to carry their own weight. They would have to be supported by a strong frame, a rigid structure as big and solid as a mountain.

Juan looked out across the fields at the solitary peak on the horizon. It was shaped like a pyramid and there was a strange circular patch near the summit. He stared more intently. Then the mountain winked at him and in surprise he fell off the lap of the girl he was sitting on and struck his head. The jolt on the boards of the porch of his house caused the gramophone needle to jump. "Cry me a river," warbled the words again, but Juan was silent.

Pontoon Bridge

They came to the wide river and wondered how they were going to cross it. Sally leaned her bicycle against a stunted tree and took out the map. "This is the River Juan," she said, "and there's a pontoon bridge about a mile in *that* direction." She pointed to the east and folded the map.

Bob frowned. "What's a pontoon bridge?"

"A floating bridge made of boats lashed together. It's a safe design that has been used for centuries, so don't worry." Sally mounted her bicycle and they set off again, pedalling along the riverbank. Soon they came to the bridge. Bob was reluctant to leave the road. He hesitated.

"Don't be scared," urged Sally. "Follow me!"

And she left him behind...

"Wait for me!" wailed Bob, following her.

It was almost sunset and mist rose from the river and blanketed everything but the effect wasn't as soft as it should be.

As they trundled over the wooden boards of the bridge, they became aware that a motorcycle was approaching from behind. It soon overtook them and came to a halt, blocking their way. The policeman dismounted and strode over to them with a grim expression. "We haven't broken any laws, have we?" squeaked Bob, but Sally nudged him quiet in the ribs.

"I'm your dealer for this evening," said the policeman.

Sally blinked. "I beg your pardon?"

"Stick or twist," said the policeman, "but be brisk about it."

"S-s-s-s-st?" stuttered Bob.

"Or twist," growled the policeman.

"Twist?" whimpered Bob.

"Twist it is!" cried the policeman and he reached into the top pocket of his jacket and flung down a playing card.

It was the Eight of Hearts. "We didn't ask for that," Sally protested.

"Yes you did. Or rather *he* did."

"All I said was 'twist?' in a baffled voice," said Bob.

"Twist again, is it? Certainly!" The policeman flung down another card, the Queen of Clubs, and Sally frowned

"But I didn't say 'twist' that time!" gasped Bob, and the policeman pulled out a third card, the Four of Diamonds.

"Bust!" declared the policeman.

"What does that—" began Sally, but the section of the bridge beneath her and Bob suddenly collapsed and they floundered in the water. The policeman leaned forwards and said in a tired voice:

"I'd love to stay and rescue you, but duty calls. I have to catch up with that car over there. Do you see it? Farewell."

In the distance, along a road perpendicular to the bridge, a rusty VW Beetle sputtered and coughed through the mist. The policeman mounted his motorcycle and set off in suitably menacing pursuit.

The City That Was Itself

You have probably never heard of Itselfia, the city that evokes only itself. Few people go there these days. That is a shame because it is rather a pleasant place, full of little squares and gardens where the inhabitants gather to play music, drink wine and forget they are lost until the following morning. Even the ruler of Itselfia can sometimes be found wandering the open spaces, asking people for directions home. Once he lived in a palace and one day he might find it again. Until that moment he satisfies himself with cheap rented accommodation.

All other cities like to dream of other cities. Itselfia does not dream or encourage dreams in its populace, unless those dreams are scenes identical to the scenes of daily urban life. Itselfia is unique. All cities are unique but the style of uniqueness possessed by Itselfia is wholly singular, for it has nothing to do with geography, architecture, the culture or character of its people. Itselfia may resemble other cities in certain aspects, the boulevards and parks and restaurants, but it refuses to acknowledge rivals. It is self-referential.

Other cities give the impression of wanting to travel elsewhere but Itselfia prefers to be only where it is. It is satisfied but not smug. Consider a city such as London. A traveller may visit London and stroll down Oxford Street and thus be reminded of Oxford; in Oxford he might cross Gloucester Green and so begin to think of Gloucester; in Gloucester he can loiter on Cheltenham Road while he daydreams of Cheltenham; in Cheltenham there is a Bath Road; in Bath an Upper Bristol Road; in Bristol a Coventry Walk; in Coventry a Norwich Drive; in Norwich a Quebec Road.

Simply by arriving in London one rainy day the traveller has already moved in some part to Canada, in terms of reference, of imagery. He is connected with places outside his actual location, and those other places are similarly connected. This process is endless and forms a gigantic loop, or rather a net that ensnares the world, for London does not evoke merely one city, Oxford, but a thousand others, each with a myriad evocations of its own. All cities are invisible lenses that diffuse a sense of place, all except the unambiguous Itselfia.

The method by which Itselfia evokes only itself is disappointingly simple. Every street, however long or short, has the same name. Likewise every square, park, building. It might be supposed that the inhabitants can still distinguish certain areas by painting houses different colours or planting trees in recognisable patterns. But without names a destination becomes merely a description, subject to inaccuracies and fatal misunderstandings. The Street of Green Houses is a new name; a street of green houses is not. The former is outlawed in Itselfia; the latter is permitted but useless.

I wanted to live in Itselfia and decided to look for work there. The journey was long and not without incident. I entered the city under the imposing arch of Itselfia Gate and walked down Itselfia Street as far as Itselfia Square. I asked for directions to Itselfia Hotel, where I planned to spend the night. I was given the same reply from many people: "Turn right or left on any corner, walk up or down any street, cross any square and knock on the door of any house." These directions were both vague and precise. I did not find my hotel. I drank wine in a garden instead.

Itselfia is not quite a labyrinth, for a labyrinth evokes other labyrinths, some with walls of stone, some with walls of thorns and leaves. Itselfia is too homely, too comfortable to be a labyrinth. When a man is lost in a labyrinth he is always where he does not wish to be. When a man is lost in Itselfia he is always in his desired place, in the right house, on the right street, listening to guitars under the right willow. It was many months before I managed to escape Itselfia. I can no longer remember if I left willingly or not. But I have never returned.

The Culture Shock

It was a museum of Doubtful Achievements and Unclear Accomplishments.

The exhibits were kept locked in glass cabinets in dimly lit galleries — achievements and accomplishments in the workplace, in domestic circumstances, at social functions, all doubtful and

137

unclear. In a room devoted to Questionable Creativity, scholars leaned on a tank of preserved fiction for a better view. The tank toppled and smashed on the floor.

The room was instantly sealed. Dr Martha Bax was summoned. "Severe outbreak of German Literature!" she was told.

"We think it's a long novel," added another.

She peered through the talent-proof window of the door. "It might mutate into something decadent. We've got to get those scholars out of there! Hold my portfolio, I'm going in!"

"Don't be a fool!" she was advised. "The Thomas Mann rating is off the scale. You'll be bored alive!"

Heeding the warning, Martha ordered an assistant to fetch a crate of beer from the nearby supermarket. "Women are more immune than men to Teutonic prose," she reasoned. "If I get blind drunk, I may be able to enter without contracting pretension"

It was a risky operation. After downing the amber liquid, she took a deep breath and entered the gallery. She staggered wildly around the room and fell over several times but eventually she managed to drag out the prone bodies of the scholars.

Later, when she had sobered up, and the contents of the gallery had been destroyed by flamethrowers, she was asked for instructions on the future of the Questionable Creativity room. Should they try to acquire a new collection? Surely it was important to preserve every expression of human culture? Clutching her head, she scowled.

"When I hear the word *culture*," she said, "I reach for my lager."

Invisible Letters

I heard her speak before I saw her, because she was on the other side of a tall library bookcase. I didn't know if she was talking directly to me: how could she know I was there? But she wasn't obviously addressing anyone else and her tone was too sweet and entreating to suggest she was talking to herself. Surely nobody is an auto-flirt?

"My name," she said, "is Mirranhgda Smyinth."

Was she foreign? "I beg your pardon?"

"I said my name is Miranda Smith," she replied.

And then there was a pause, and I realised I was expected to reveal my own name in return, like exchanging sweets from a bag, a gobstopper for a humbug. "And I am Jhohdnn Brrouwlln."

"John Brown, did you say? How do you do!"

I nodded, even though she couldn't see the gesture. Then I had an urge to gaze on her, so I began circling the bookcase, but she patently had the same idea, because she stepped round to where I had been, and that's how we missed each other, and kept doing so.

"Are you baffled?" she asked me, and then added, "Not by the fact the bookcase is still between us, because that's a matter of geometry, timing, velocity and other physical variables, but by the silent letters that festoon my name? Most people I meet are."

"There are silent letters in my name too," I answered.

Maybe my tone was a touch defiant because she laughed lightly and at once my heart leapt in my chest. She said:

"Yes, but my silent letters can occasionally be heard."

"Then they aren't silent!" I cried, before adding more delicately, "The same is true for me: they make some noise."

"What do you think this means?" she asked softly.

I shrugged: another unseen gesture.

"Do you suppose," she added teasingly, "that silent letters have started to assert themselves in the world at last?"

I smiled at this curious notion, her quaint and surely ironic conceit that letters might have consciousness and a deliberate purpose, that they might feel resentment and determination; but I decided to humour her. The truth is that I found her voice attractive and so—

But no, a voice reveals nothing of deep insight about the appearance or character of a woman; it's a false clue, as unreliable as bumps on the head or astrological signs or handwriting style.

"Feasibly they have," I announced, "and doubtless they will insist on enjoying equal rights with all non-silent letters, so the 'p' in 'pterodactyl' will henceforth be pronounced on every tongue that utters the name of the creature, but very little will alter in the grand scheme of things. I know a few people already who say, 'pterodactyl.'"

"Do you truly believe the outcome will be so easy?"

She was serious now, that much was clear. I changed my direction and tried to catch her by circling the bookcase anti-clockwise but it turned out that she had reversed her direction too.

"This phenomenon…" I began in a sharper voice.

"No, it's more deliberate than that. It's a rebellion. The silent letters in my name were once only heard two or three times a year by strangers, but now they are heard more often than not."

I sighed in mild exasperation. "A general surge into audibility of silent letters will lead to an official review of the language by those experts who compile dictionaries. After all, it's their responsibility, not ours. Spelling will be simplified and the rebellious letters edited away into oblivion. The danger won't be as severe as you imagine."

"What if they are only the vanguard? What about—"

She chuckled and I knew she was toying with me, but I didn't care. In fact I thought I understood her properly now. She was a prankster, maybe a student from the local university, relieving the boredom of a bland grey day with an absurdist joke, a madcap routine.

I responded to her challenge. "What about what?"

"What about invisible letters?"

"And what are those but letters that don't exist?"

I stopped circling the bookcase. Would she come to me instead? But it appeared she had paused at the exact same instant, perhaps to take a book from a shelf and open it at a random page.

"They do exist. Listen. We accept letters that are visible but silent. We may not like them, but we don't refuse them; they are a quirky feature of language, we know them, we have made lists; but consider letters that are invisible and equally silent. What if they too decide to assert themselves, to become visible and also make a noise?"

"That is a pointless anxiety. There are no such things."

"Look! Open a book, any book…"

Compelled by the urgency of her tone, by its mocking undercurrents, I pulled out the nearest volume and opened it. The text was unreadable, an atrocious writhing mess of compressed letters. I was knocked backwards by the force of the sonic boom as they detonated; and I dropped the book as I vainly struggled to maintain my balance.

"See?" she shouted, and there was only compassion in her voice now, and resignation, and a touch of melancholy. "There were always far more invisible letters in every word than visible ones. Hundreds, thousands and millions of them for each visible word!"

I said nothing. The titles embossed on the spines of every book I gazed at had become gibberish; letters dripped from them onto the floor, slowly at first but with increasing velocity, becoming a trickle, a gush, a cataract that filled the library and rose higher and higher, the bookshelves floating on the ocean of dismembered words like rafts.

I clung to one, but the woman wasn't with me. I was alone. The doors burst open with the pressure and out I went, riding a current of verbosity along the streets to the door of my house.

And this is a true s s s s s s t t t t t t t t o o o o o o r r r r r r r y y y y y y.

Making a Request

"Why don't you ever come to Wales?" asked the people of that country, through a gigantic megaphone that penetrated the thick endless layers of low grey cloud. "Not once in living memory have you visited us; but we have many attractions for you to shine on! There are castles and hills and forests and secret valleys and little offshore islands and ancient megaliths and the ruins of abbeys and quaint piers and narrow-gauge railways and rousing choirs and coracles and odd hats. Take a copy of this guide book and read about them for yourself!"

"Don't be silly!" came the muffled reply. "How can I read anything if I have no eyes? How can I hear what you are saying, or respond to it, if I have no ears or mouth? I'm not even a sentient being but an unimaginably vast ball of seething hydrogen and helium atoms. So go away and leave me alone. Your request is foolish!"

The sun will use any excuse to avoid Wales.

Eggs

He hated eggs, absolutely hated them, but his wife gave them to him for breakfast every morning. "I hate eggs!" he snapped at her, but it seemed she wasn't listening, because she continued to cook them in a heavy pan smeared with grease that was yellow like rancid pus. He banged his knife down on the table. "Did you hear me?"

It was raining outside and the dreary raindrops fell on the grimy panes of the warped windows that looked out on a barren garden where all the grass had died. There had been a chicken coop out there once, he recalled, but it was gone now. That was funny. Not funny ha ha but funny peculiar. The eggs sizzled in the pan like hornets.

In the grey light that filled the gloomy room, he was unable to read the newspaper without squinting. The newspaper was printed in grey ink that was as depressing and faded as the sky. The headlines made no sense, but it seemed that the price of eggs had gone up. There were no chickens left anywhere on any farms. The rain pelted.

"I don't want eggs for breakfast," he said patiently, "I want an onion, a roll and some coffee instead." But she didn't heed him and he felt like he was crushed under the weight of the hissing yolk in the pan. He wanted to scream and run away but there was nowhere to run to because every place in the entire world was utterly like this one.

He chewed his lower lip. Despite his hatred of eggs he was hungry. A dull thumping began somewhere in his brain. "Are those eggs ready yet? I don't want them but I must have them," he cried. She walked up to him with the saucepan held out in front of her. Then she hit him on the crown of the head with it. "Here they are!" she said.

His head crackled like a shell, precisely like an eggshell, and the yolk of his brains trickled down his face and onto his protruding tongue. Then at last he knew what he was. He was chicken. Too chicken to confront the reality of his doom. A henpecked husband. And she was a ghost or some sort of psycho. He knew all this and then died.

Volcano Zoo

"There are no extinct volcanoes in our country," said the zookeeper, "because our government was wise enough to capture a few and keep them in captivity before they died out. We plan to let them breed and when there are enough we will release them back into the wild."

"Won't the farmers and villagers object to that?"

"Our geology is our heritage."

I walked past the cages where the cones fumed and rumbled. The yellow vapours coiled and danced. I lit a match.

The zookeeper rushed up, his face bright purple, and knocked the pipe out of my mouth and onto the ground.

"Can't you read the signs? NO SMOKING!"

In My Own Hands

I took my life into my own hands.

But my life was contained in my entire body, so I took my entire body into my own hands.

My own hands are part of my entire body.

So I took my own hands into my own hands.

But my own hands were already holding my entire body, including my own hands, which were holding my entire body, including my own hands, which were holding my entire body, including my own hands, and so on forever, so there simply wasn't any room.

Damn those figures of speech!

Daggers

She was looking daggers at me.

I reached across, grasped one of the daggers by its rosewood hilt, drew it out of her glare with a faint musical note and used it to cut a wedge of cheese on the plate before me.

"How dare you slice food with my fury?" she cried.

I stomped off to my room.

Hammer, saw, nails, planks of wood... Every time I make my bed I ask myself, "What if I've misunderstood something?"

Cosmic Bagatelle

The city was finished just in time. The last of the towers was raised an hour before the deadline. We sat on the grass, agitated but disciplined, to watch. We savaged dainty sandwiches with our broken teeth and quaffed flasks of perfumed tea.

The asteroid had been detected a month earlier. Emperor Chi-Twing had made the announcement. It would strike the heart of the kingdom. There was only one thing to do. We quarried stone, erected scaffolding, mortared bricks with sweat and blood.

The city was constructed on a sloping plain. Astronomers worked out the point of impact. A vast spring, smelted from every sword, scythe and earring in the land, was coiled into position. The towers were arranged in semi-circles and filled with peasants.

The asteroid struck the spring just before noon. It bounced once and rolled up the plain. At the top it collided with the city wall and began to roll down again.

We watched the progress of the spherical mass as it crashed against the first of the towers, dislodging occupants from windows. The edifice deflected it away from one of the low-value crescents and into the most inaccessible corner.

****** 100 POINTS! ******

As the peasants in that quarter were marched off to execution, the Emperor sent a message to us by carrier-tortoise. We had drawn with the Chang-Twang dynasty. A giant catapult was to be constructed immediately, to hurl the thing back into space.

It was all on the tie-break.

A Post-Disaster Story

Scientists had no way of stopping the asteroid. A postal worker had an idea. He went into space in a rocket and fixed a stamp to it. Now it was the responsibility of the Post Office. They typically failed to deliver it correctly. It struck Mars. The Earth was saved.

NOTE: The above story is an example of a microfiction sub-genre called the 'Mini-Saga'. The idea is to write a complete short story with a beginning, middle and end in exactly 50 words. The title is not included in the word count but shouldn't exceed 15 words.

Pretty Face
(another mini-saga)

He would do anything for a pretty face. When his wife caught him stealing her makeup there was a struggle. She fell and hit her head on the bedside cabinet. He went to fetch the scissors. And now he wears her face over his own and it *is* pretty. Awful.

In Eclipseville

In Eclipseville the authorities have decreed that shadows are more real than the objects that cast them. Substances have no value there: the people would spit on them if spit weren't also a substance.

Some grades of shadow are more highly regarded than others; this goes without saying. The shadows of watermelons have great status, as do those of clocks, scissors, tall hats. The most valuable shade of all remains to be seen: the shadow of the sun.

Not all shadows are visual. The authorities insist that musical notes are the true shadows of instruments, rather than those outlines that pretend to be flutes, harps, dulcimers. The implications of this creed seem absurd to outsiders. Cymbals are only symbols of their own tinkle.

In Eclipseville most nocturnal activities take place in the afternoon. Between lunch and teatime, night watchmen poke about in cellars for evidence of the night, in accordance with their contracts of employment, but never find any until they abandon the search and switch off their electric torches.

Meanwhile lovers perspire, servants worry about ghosts, burglars prowl, lurkers throb, pools of wax on tablecloths harden under stubs of candles in closed cafés, astronomers squint through lenses on rooftops and insomniacs generate soft piano music or gently pluck the strings of muted lutes while uncultured neighbours snore.

Many of those talented insomniacs learned to play in the famous Music Institute, a building that is the grandest on the urban landscape. In truth it is not a single structure but a cluster of dwellings sheltered by a translucent dome, a difference that is a question of interpretation, for a sweet melody might likewise be defined as a sequence of unrelated notes linked 'only' by a key signature.

Some say the mansion of Frabjal Troose is one of those clustered dwellings; not I. Others say the Once Held Hands Crossing is also contained within the Institute; I disagree again.

My name is Sacerdotal Bagge and I'm one of the authorities of the city. My disagreements are shadowy, like my policies, but I remain undisturbed, for not all shadows are dark. One day a brighter star will move behind the sun and the sun will drape its own shadow, blinkingly bright, on our houses, souls and financial affairs.

Let it be known that Eclipseville had a difficult birth, for it was the result of a collision and meshing between two contradictory forces, the cities of Moonville and Sunsetville. When the moon passes before the sun the day becomes night, and wine, kisses, oddness and nocturnes are suddenly necessary. An expensive business…

An attempt was once made to freeze one of our best shadows. A hat taller than the highest minaret

149

was positioned so that its shadow fell into a vat of liquid hydrogen. The procedure worked. When the hat was removed its shadow remained in the cold fluid.

But the shadow was brittle and when it was fished out it shattered into a million fragments. These splinters were caught up by the wind and swirled down the streets. Some specks lodged in the eyes of men and women; others stabbed into hearts.

With those motes blurring their vision, the citizens of Eclipseville saw hats everywhere. Teapot lids became sombreros, manhole covers turned into berets, even eyelids were perceived as being skullcaps for eyeballs. As for people with hat shards in their cardiac muscles, they soon found themselves brimming over, but not always with emotion.

Although a success, the experiment was deemed a failure. That is often the case in Eclipseville, and I, Sacerdotal Bagge, have little desire to change our methodology. In fact I backed the decision to make a second attempt, to freeze an aural shadow instead of a visual one, to solidify a musical note. We constructed a special machine. A hearing trumpet of immense size led into the side of a gigantic compression refrigerator.

A lever worked gears that lowered extremely heavy weights onto a piston. But first we needed something to compress. Musicians came and played the same note into the mouth of the trumpet and when the inner chamber was full I pulled the lever.

Slowly the sound was crushed into an enormous black orb. The chamber was opened. Inside: solid music, smooth, humming faintly but insistently. What did we do with it? We launched it into space with a catapult, fixed it to the line of the celestial equator. A note belongs on a stave. Only there will it play properly.

Imagine many spheres of solid music in orbit, pinned by gravity to the ecliptic and other lines of heavenly latitude. An authentic prelude to the future...

The globe orbited our planet like a swollen drone, crossing in front of the sun and the real moon, increasing the frequency of eclipses visible from our city, but it did not play for us. There is no sound in a vacuum. No matter. The note was visible. We imagined it would remain in place forever, but it began to fade. The same note sustained too long becomes inaudible. We had forgotten that simple fact.

Eventually it was gone. We didn't care.

A big mistake. Just because an object is invisible doesn't mean it has ceased to exist. Then something very unexpected occurred. A delegation from a brighter star crashed into the note without realising it was there and was destroyed. They had planned to offer us admission to a galactic club of advanced civilisations. The attendant benefits were consumed in plasma flames. For long minutes shadows held no sway.

The authorities of Eclipseville no longer emerge from their offices but shamefully project their shadows out of little rooms over the thresholds of doorways, down marble steps, into the streets. They wag long flat fingers on flagstones, wavy fingers on cobbles.

These fingers form a musical stave. Shards of a broken moon fall on the lines or between them. Such things must happen in a city where one strange event is always eclipsed by another.

Owls Are a Hoot

I saw a dead rainbow on the street when I was walking home today. People told me it was just an oil spill but I knew what it was...

People tell me that owls are a hoot but I don't believe them.

When I was younger I lived with a pun. People said that I ought to live with a woman instead, but I didn't. The pun liked going out.

One evening it went to the theatre to see a play — a wordplay.

"The performance was a joke," it told me later.

I didn't believe that. People told me that I should believe it. I refused.

I saw a dead baby ghost on the street when I was walking home today. People told me it was just a discarded handkerchief but I knew what it was...

A Pony Tale

"The girl tied back her long hair," said the young horse.

THE END

Gorgon but Not Forgotten

What if all Ancient Greek statutes are actually victims of Medusa and the other Gorgons? This was a question that occurred to me once and I shared it with a friend of mine who is a sculptor.

"It's not possible. The internal organs would be turned to stone too and when such a statue is broken open it reveals nothing of the sort. I have never seen petrified lungs or liver inside one."

I couldn't argue with his answer and I went away, but something in his expression bothered me and continued to do so. I sneaked back later and spied through his window as he worked. He was creating a forgery, something that could be broken open without arousing suspicion.

Then I saw the shadows of snakes.

I fled and now I avoid his studio. He must have a heart of stone to work willingly for one of those monsters.

The Sink Monster

"There is a monster in the sink," David said to his mother over breakfast one morning when he was finally unable to bear the tension any longer. A man who wore tension like armour, David had been brought up without a father and didn't even know what a flat cap was. But he was familiar with soap and the other adjuncts of washing.

"Don't be a brat! You are an abomination!" his mother screeched from the lowest point of the sagging curve of her wheelchair seat. It was more than ninety years old, her contraption, and she hadn't been disabled when she'd first sat on it to try it out; but the seat had collapsed under her and it had trapped her

153

153

there ever since, in the same way that a desire might be trapped inside a repression like a seed.

"Yes, mummy. Sorry, mummy," David said obediently.

But there *was* a monster in the sink.

He saw it every time he went to wash his hands.

Clearing away the breakfast tray and scraping the remains of the eggs that his mother had devoured like a beast out of the window and onto the compost heap, which shifted as if it was alive, David finished washing up and tramped slowly down the passage to the stairs; then he went up these creaking steps and into the bathroom.

"Why doesn't mummy love me? Shall I kill her?"

He spoke with both taps turned full on to disguise his words. Although he hadn't put the plug in yet, the force of the water was so great that the sink filled up anyway. The waters swirled like a miniature whirlpool and then something stirred in the chaotic depths. What was it? David peered closer. A finger emerged from the froth.

"It's beckoning me! Like a beckoning fair one!"

He leaned forward. And then a damp hand was thrust out and grabbed him by the tie his mother insisted that he always wear, even when he was nude. The hand began reeling him in. "No!" he screamed. "No!" gargled he. But it was too late, or too early, or something. Nobody was available to help anywhere. He was pulled inside.

Down the plughole he went, spinning like a rotating thing. What was the monster that was about to devour him?

154

In the final instant before his demise, David saw—

The horror! A man's cloth cap!

Geronimo

Three college girls were baring their behinds out of the dormitory window on the night my parachute jump went wrong.

And they say the moon landings were faked?

I Saw a Ghost Ship

I saw a ghost ship in a bottle of spirits, a rum tale to mull over on a long walk home; I saw a reindeer with a flashing nose jumping the red light of the setting sun; I saw a seasonal robin with a bag of swag flapping out of the nearest bank. Oh dear! What next? A white-bearded man on the roof of a house, coming down with the flue; the woolly members of a closely-knit family needling each other. Surely none of it could be true? As the turkey once said when we cracked its wishbone, "Are you pulling my leg?"

The Tribal Philosophers

The people of the remote island said to each other, "The light of the moon is more important than the light of the sun. This isn't hard to believe! The light of the moon appears at night, when it's most needed; but the light of the sun appears only in the daytime, when we can already see everything clearly, and is therefore superfluous."

And they added salt and pepper to the missionary.

Stale Air

They had been stuck indoors all week, Toby and Gerrold, and so they decided to go for a nice walk on Sunday afternoon. But first they went to the pub for lunch and a few pints of ale. By the time they set off again the sky was clouding over and the path through the woods seemed less enticing than before.

Toby stopped in his tracks and yawned. "I'm so tired!"

"It's all the fresh air," said Gerrold.

"Let's find somewhere to sit, shall we? How about over here?"

"In the graveyard?" asked Gerrold.

"Yes. That tombstone looks comfortable enough. The light will be fading in about an hour. After our rest we should turn back."

They scuffed through loose earth to reach the tombstone. They removed their jackets to make cushions and dangled their legs. Toby yawned again and Gerrold followed his example. "Too much fresh air!" they chorused.

Gerrold opened his knapsack and removed two plastic bags. The first contained four cans of ale, the second held a packet of tobacco, rolling papers, a box of filters and a lighter. They both yawned again.

"I don't understand," began Toby.

"What don't you understand?" pressed Gerrold. A can of ale hissed in his hand as he opened it. Before he could take a sip, he yawned.

Toby yawned as well. Contagious.

"Why fresh air should make a person yawn. Fresh, mind you. *Fresh*!"

"It's what happens," explained Gerrold.

"I know that. But why?"

Gerrold shrugged. "Too much of a good thing is bad, maybe?"

Toby yawned. "It goes against logic."

"I suppose it does, but it's what people say all the time. 'The fresh air is making me tired!' It's just one of the paradoxes of life."

"It implies that stale air makes you more active," pointed out Toby.

"Yes it does," conceded Gerrold.

"And where might you find the stalest air?" pressed Toby.

Gerrold considered. "Inside a damaged submarine lying at the bottom of the sea full of suffocating men. Those doomed crews must be *very* active!"

"Or inside the coffin of a person buried alive?" suggested Toby.

"There too," said Gerrold.

They glanced at the loose earth they had recently stepped on. Now they realised there was a peculiar odour hanging over the graveyard, the smell of dampness, mould, severed worms, mothballs and diseased flesh. A burial had taken place not long ago. And there was a scraping noise, a subterranean rumble, faint but growing louder.

157

"If fresh air makes you tired, stale air must make you more wakeful, more active, stronger," reiterated Toby, "so if you are accidentally buried alive, your physical power must increase as your air turns foul. Eventually you will become strong enough to burst out of your grave. It stands to reason, doesn't it?"

The ground erupted in front of them. A pseudo-corpse stood there, rictus rage on its sallow features, splinters of shattered coffin on the shoulders of its musty suit, its entire frame shaking with malignant energy.

"Run!" yelled Toby and Gerrold.

After a few seconds they collapsed exhausted. "We're too tired to flee!" wailed Toby. "All the fresh air has sapped our vitality. The monster will catch us!"

Gerrold shook his head with considerable effort. "No it won't. It's no longer surrounded by stale air and has lost its vitality too!"

Toby looked back and saw that Gerrold had spoken the truth. The fake zombie was leaning against the tombstone for support, yawning madly.

"But what's it doing?" shrieked Toby.

"I left my tobacco behind!" lamented Gerrold. "It's rolling itself a cigarette!"

The click of the lighter was audible.

"When it cleans the fresh air out of its lungs it will be once more active enough to pursue us. We are finished!" sobbed Toby.

"We have only one chance. We need to return to the tombstone and snatch back the two plastic bags. If we put them over our heads and start to asphyxiate we will regain enough energy to outdistance the grotesque fiend!"

"Yes, let's do that!" croaked Toby.

"On second thoughts, why bother? This is a very silly story."

"Yes it is," confirmed Toby.

The Sun Lamp

Two merchants approached the sun and said, "We have something to sell you that we know you'll find very useful. In this box is the latest kind of sun lamp! It's powerful and projects a light similar to your own. So now you'll be able to read books or comb your hair or search for dropped pins or squeeze your spots at night."

The sun frowned. "I don't know what you mean."

The merchants smiled indulgently. "Which part don't you understand? The books, the comb or the pins?"

And the sun answered, "What is night?"

The Falling Lover

(1) She said: This is how it happened, walking down the street, over the bridge, three shopping bags clutched in my right hand, two in my left, a fine imbalance, I leant like a toothpick in a glass, my bright yellow and orange hair fanned out in the wind, the handles of the bags cut into my palms, buses passed me swirling leaves, under the crumbling tenements of the estate he leapt on me.

Leapt on me, oh yes, full of passion from the tenth floor, holding his nose like a diver plunging into a barrel, kissed my brow with his velocity lips, could not even elucidate a gasp, just knocked me over, we tumbled and rolled together, limbs knotted, my skirt hitched above my thighs, we rolled to the feet of an old man waiting at the bus stop, he struck us with his umbrella and cried, "What's the world coming to?"

(2) He said: This is how it happened, standing on my balcony, watering my plants, suddenly knew it was pointless, opened my heart to the landscape, tried to love the world, found my current philosophy inadequate, the city held a strange beauty, a fossil petrified by its own excretions, it was the sort of beauty I could not face, I had cut myself shaving that morning, blood on the mirror, on my pale hands, the same sort of beauty, unreasonable, unnecessary.

I climbed over the railings, holding my genitals like a man about to be hung, toppled over without a murmur, struck a woman with my chin, cried out loudly in shame, knocked her down, rolled faster and faster, the velcro fastenings on my jacket stuck to her cardigan, I could not disentangle, her trousers were torn, we stopped at the feet of an old man waiting at the bus stop, he made a gesture with his umbrella and cried, "Give her one for me, son."

(3) I said: This is how it happened, cold day as always, aching knees, each minute like a short stretch of canal, flat, uninspiring, used to work the locks myself, the aftertaste of lunch on withered tongue, warmed up from the previous day, somehow different, decided to catch a bus into town, throttle afternoon in the concrete Mall, walked to the bus

stop, counted my change, saw a man throwing himself out of a window, holding his ear like a liar with lobes of gold.

Down he fell, struck a woman with his nose, rolled with her towards me, her shorts caked with mud, stopped at my feet and giggled, I cried, "Why wallow in bad faith, debase yourself before reality, dwell in a quietism of despair? Why betray absurdity, choose not to choose, abandon abandonment? Don't you know that the sclerosis of objectivity is the annihilation of existence, that masturbation is merely a congealing of reveries? Stand and fight!" I gestured with my hands alone, I had no umbrella, I admire and wish to emulate rain.

The Imp of the Icebox

Behind the tomatoes, under the lettuce, lurks the imp of the icebox. He alone knows that the fridge light stays on when the door is closed. His lips are salty with brine; at night he dips his twisted fingers into the olive jar. He used to live in a pantry, chuckling silent from cobweb depths, climbing between the tree-like growths of forgotten potatoes, counting the rust spots on kitchen knives, pulling the tails of frightened mice in the pre-dawn dark. But all that was long ago. Times have changed. In the sterile, ugly fridge he shivers and chatters in grudging progress.

Cold womb, frost goddess, snow mother, barren and hard, chill me with your icy breath. I listen to the beat of your motor heart, hear the gurgling of your Freon circulation. I roll the softest fruits into the furthest corners, make my bed on the down of a

161

mouldy peach. The aubergine is my chateau, the cheese my moon. Hot radish burns my tongue, I swim breaststroke in the gravy boat, slide a churn through the butterdish. There is all here I could ever desire, and more. But I am lonely. I miss the company. I miss the larder. The slugs and the green spiders. I miss them all...

Virgil Leading Dante into Hell Takes a Wrong Turning

They had arrived at last. The concentric circles spread out before them like ripples in a lake. Filthy water, Stygian water, glittered darkly. The machines of torment rotated slowly in the distance, huge arms sweeping across the polluted sky.

Brueghel himself could not have imagined a more ghastly scene. A trio of grinning figures, obviously demons, exhaled noxious fumes from tubes clenched between their teeth. Other malevolent creatures cowered in the shadows, gibbering and snarling.

And yet, there was something wrong. Something not quite right. He scratched his head and tried to fathom the meaning. The place certainly stank, the howls matched his ideas exactly. Sinners in abundance there were too, lost souls moving towards them.

But why were they all mounted on bicycles?

"Are we really in the Netherworlds?" he asked suddenly, bravely squinting forward into all the horror.

"The Netherworlds?" His guide frowned and

shuffled uneasily. "The Netherworlds?" He lowered his gaze and cleared his throat. "I see. Then there has been a slight misunderstanding…"

"Well?"

"I thought you said the Netherlands."

The Precious Mundanity

After the boy was tucked up snugly in bed, the mother kissed his forehead but she didn't turn to leave. Then the boy said, "I'm so excited about tomorrow I don't think I'll ever get to sleep!"

She smiled at him and patted the sheets, but her face was sad. "There's something I need to tell you," she said.

His eyes widened in response. "You don't mean I'm not adopted?"

"Don't be silly." She laughed. "Why would I lie about that? You've always known my husband isn't your real father. No, it's something else. You're seven years old now and it's time you learned the truth."

"I don't understand, mother," he answered.

She sighed and regarded the simple bedroom. They were a poor family and lived in a very modest house in a shabby town. Outside, the sun had already set, but the sky still held enough light to illuminate the people trudging up the dusty street. A donkey began braying and kicking a clay wall; elsewhere the tradesmen and merchants were shutting their shops. A pale moon rose over the low hills. A normal evening.

"It's about Christmas," she said.

He was sitting up in bed now, blinking at her. "Yes?"

"Father Christmas in particular..."

His eyes lit up at the mention of this name. "Last year he brought me a toy boat and the year before that he gave me a ball and the year before that..." He caught his breath and added, "I can't wait to see what he'll give me tomorrow!"

She placed a finger over his lips and shook her head. "That's exactly what I must tell you. Father Christmas doesn't actually exist. It's your father who brings you those gifts. Your real father. That's the truth."

"What?" He was distraught. "You mean there's no such thing as Santa Claus? The jolly fat man in red with a sack over his shoulder is just a myth? A lie?"

"I'm afraid so. Your father pretends to be him."

"My father? My real father? The supernatural force that created the universe? The omniscient, omnipotent lord of everything? Oh mother! You've turned Christmas into a magical occasion. You've destroyed the mundanity of it! The precious mundanity! I'll never forgive you for this. Never!"

"My poor son," She reached out to hug him close to her, but he pounded his little fists against her and then fell back on the bed and turned on his side. She spoke to his bristling back. "I'm sorry to break the news this way. Santa Claus is from the future, you see. That's why your father keeps up the pretence. Even Christmas hasn't been invented yet!"

But it was no use. He wasn't listening. She rose and quietly left Jesus sobbing into his pillow.

164

The Earthworm's Ecstasy

The ecstasy of the earthworm lay in its dreams of above. Its world was the rich warm earth that surrounded and enclosed it, caressed and passed through it. Life was good but a feeling remained unsatisfied. It wanted to see above for itself. The other worms disapproved. Better to know nothing about above, they said. Many even denied its existence. The few who claimed to have been there warned of a heavy piercing light and a reality beyond understanding. They described their frantic attempts to burrow back down into the rich soil. They told of fellow worms that had reached above and had never returned. Yet these tales could not prevent the yearning.

Did above truly exist or was it merely a myth for wormlings? It had to know. The way to above lay where the soil grew thin and where the roots thickened. So it resolved to say farewell to its friends and begin the journey the next morning. As soon as it had made this resolution, a miracle happened. The earth shook and a huge metal blade descended through it, tossing its front end into another dimension. There was woodsmoke and a frosty rime. Although its brain could hold no concept of the swooping blackbird, its friends beneath were able to mumble platitudes to its other half for weeks.

Moonchaser

In most cultures throughout human history the moon has been regarded as a feminine body. So what is the

Man in the Moon doing there? The obvious, I suppose...

The cycles of the moon always bewilder me and I can never seem to predict when it is going to rise. I even have difficulty guessing where on the landscape it will choose to appear. It nearly always catches me out, jumping up so rapidly that it has already cleared the horizon before I notice its existence. Then it shifts gears and slows down, sliding up the dome of the sky like an object deliberately losing momentum.

Why don't I possess the same instinct for the movements of the moon as I do for those of the sun? It is peculiar.

I hurry to attend my lecture in astrobiology, a science I never knew existed until I found myself studying it accidentally last month. The college is a hallowed building, so hallowed it has fallen down in some places and swollen upwards in others, implausibly.

My lecturer is Professor Krator and his spectacles twinkle as he regards the students on the rows of tiered seats. "Now I'm going to tell you a secret truth that very few people know. It will explain why you find it so difficult to predict the moon's movements and why it looks bigger on some nights than others. There is not just one moon but two, a female *and* a male. The male moon is constantly chasing the female."

"Really?" we all gasp. "But why?"

"Why do you think? For reasons of physical desire. If he ever catches her, you can be sure that baby moons will be the result, a dozen of them. And when they all grow to full size the tidal effects will be dreadful. As for moths and lovers: utter confusion!"

166

He pedals away after the lecture on a bicycle with inflatable moons instead of wheels. Perhaps he is eccentric.

The students are required to devise their own projects in their spare time in order to achieve a high grade. I decide to trap the female moon in a net to give the male moon the chance to reach her. I walk down to the harbour and hire a number of nets from the fishermen and tie them together. Then I hike up into the mountains and string them between two peaks where the moon often passes.

I wait in the foothills for nightfall. Sure enough, shortly after sunset, the moon appears in the east. I assume it is the female moon and that the male moon is somewhere behind her, but as it happens my timing is wrong. It is the stronger male moon that sails into the net, stretching it almost to snapping point.

But the mesh doesn't break. Instead it catapults the moon back from whence it came. I groan in dismay, for I know Professor Krator will mark me down for reversing the direction of the moon's orbit. It vanishes back over the eastern horizon at the same instant that the previously unnoticed female moon sets over the western.

They will meet and collide on the far side of the world, but then what? Sure enough a dull booming sound rises up through the ground and vibrates my legs and my skeleton.

Thousands of baby moons swarm into the night sky from every direction. Thousands? But Professor Krator insisted that a female moon never gave birth to more than a dozen.

Then I realise the truth. "It's all my fault!"

The two adult moons have shattered into fragments, misshapen pieces that are grotesque parodies of newborn moons. I return home with a doleful expression. Although these fragments aren't proper moons they act as if they are and the tidal effects are rather strange.

Whereas two intact moons had produced two big tides every day, in the oceans of the world, several thousand miniature moons produce several thousand miniature tides in the same space of time, but in bodies of liquid that are appropriately small. There are now tides in places where they could never be found before. In my kitchen sink, my teacup, my mouth.

My fellow students and all other citizens mostly shun me. One day I watch a large fragment fall into the sea. When I paddle my canoe to a point directly above it and thrust my head under the surface for a closer look, I see that the meteorite is actually two conjoined parts: two sets of stone lips in the act of kissing.

I do consider raising them in my net despite the immense weight, but what sense is there in fishing for mouths?

The Jeweller

There was a girl who took crystals and wrapped them in wire and twisted the wire into elaborate patterns, so the crystals could be hung from little chains and worn around the neck.

In the sunlight, these crystals shone with many colours.

"What are you up to?" asked the sun, as it passed overhead. "What are you doing with those sparkly things?"

"I'm making pedants," answered the girl.

"Pedants? I think you mean *pendants*," corrected the sun.

The girl smiled. "Yes, those too."

Fairy Dusk

Anna waded through the tall grasses of the meadow until she reached the highest point of the ridge. Then she opened the folding chair she had been carrying under one arm and set up the easel she had been carrying under the other. From a rucksack she extracted a canvas and positioned it on the easel. Finally she sat down gleefully.

"Where are your brush and paints?" Gareth asked.

He had preceded her by almost one hour. He was perched on a folding chair of his own and a canvas stood in front of him, balanced on an easel. Hooked on his left thumb was a traditional palette covered in overlapping circles of acrylic paint. He scratched at his nose with the rear end of his brush and blinked at Anna suspiciously.

"Oh, I don't need those things," she replied blithely.

"But how," he cried, indicating his own work in progress, a picture of the valley below, "are you going to paint this vista without them? I asked you to come painting with me this evening: paint is required to make the pastime work. A palette is also required and you don't appear to have one of those either. I think you are inept."

"Don't worry." She waved a dismissive hand.

He frowned. The sun was setting at the end of the valley and the long shadows of the trees made everything seem extra true and special. Soon it would be twilight and then dusk; there wasn't much time to try to capture the magic of the scene. He dipped the tip of his brush in an oval puddle of orange and dabbed a corner of his canvas.

Anna still made no effort to begin work. Gareth scowled at her and she said, "I don't plan on painting it myself."

"What do you mean by that?"

"Do you remember that company based in Cork, in Eire? Little People Inc. Well, I contacted them and asked them to send me some fairies to do the task for me. I gave them this location and explained that I wanted to paint the valley but couldn't be bothered to do so. No problem, they said. Fairies are very conscientious artists."

"That's just plain lazy."

"It makes perfect sense to me."

Gareth muttered something unintelligible and returned to his painting, but as he proceeded he became aware that his artwork no longer matched the reality of the view. The clouds in front of the sun weren't orange any more but lime green! How the heck—?

The sun itself was changing colour. Purple and yellow vertical stripes with black and white dots. As it set, the stripes were left behind and they gradually darkened and broadened until they covered half the western sky while the dots plopped down onto the ground and spread over the unseen rocks and grass of the valley bottom.

The light was fading fast. Buzzing creatures were flitting about faster than the eye could register and wherever they passed the skyglow turned murkier and thicker. Dusk was early.

Anna stood up quickly, knocking over her easel. She waved at the tiny creatures and then gestured at her toppled canvas. "On here, you fools! I wanted you to paint the valley on *this*!"

Bunch of Oddballs

The dying planet spoke first to the star it orbited and then to its own atmosphere. "You are my sun and air," it said.

"Who gets your humans?" they asked.

"I never got them myself. Bunch of oddballs," replied the planet.

The Apricot Jar

She instructs him not to eat any of the dried apricots that she has placed in a jar on the windowsill, but he is sorely tempted. He licks his lips and wonders whether her anger will be real if he takes an apricot, or whether it will be illusory. Perhaps she will merely give a knowing laugh and forgive him. Or perhaps she will cleanse his image from her perfect green eyes, those emeralds of Arcadia, those olives of desire. He is confused. There is no advice he can seek on this problem. His friends do not know enough about the subject and professional help is too expensive. He makes a tour of the charities, but none deal with the apricot question. He begins to feel the weight of a fruity despair.

Inside the jar, the apricots linger. He reaches for the jar and then lets his hand drop back down. The decision is entirely his own responsibility. He suddenly realises that if he eats an apricot, he is serving as a model for the whole human race. Every man and woman is allowed to eat a secret apricot. If, on the other hand, he refrains, then he is validating the non-eating of apricots for everyone. He is validating the collapse of the apricot industry. He finally decides to accept the consequences, and he eats an apricot. And now he lives in a jar, with no other company than the apricots of regret...

Deluged With Aunts

This next story is rather more sombre and perverse. We have a loner who lives in a garret, or a bedsit, and who never speaks to any of the other tenants in the building. He has no close family (they have all died in mysterious and truly grisly circumstances) but he is deluged with aunts. There is Aunt Emily and Aunt Theresa and Aunt Hilda and Aunt Eva. At the funerals of his mother or father or brothers or sisters, they each take it in turns to mumble such platitudes as "you have your father's eyes" or "you have your mother's nose" or "you have your sister's ears" or some such thing. The loner merely nods and purses his lips. Once back in his tiny room, he digs up the floorboards and removes the plastic bags concealed there. He is all despair. "How do they know?" he wails.

The Sundial

"I wonder what time it is?" the sun said as it passed over a land where trees were dropping fruit. There was no one to ask; but then it spotted a sundial in an overgrown garden. "I just need to consult this delightful contrivance and then I'll know."

But it came away frustrated.

"Typical! The part that holds the information is the one part that's in shadow and I can't see a thing!"

Better the Devil

"Better the devil," said Samuel.

"Meaning what exactly?" I asked.

"Better the one you know than the one you don't," he replied.

"But I don't know *any* devils," I said.

He laughed. "Yes you do. We all do. We all know THE Devil. Satan, I mean. Lucifer. The Prince of Hell."

"Actually, I don't know him," I pointed out.

"He knows you," Samuel said.

I winced. "Even if I concede the point and admit that I know one devil, it still doesn't mean you are right."

He grinned and showed his cracked teeth.

"It's folk wisdom, my friend. The knowledge of our ancestors. I'm sure they knew what they were talking about. The devil we know is better than the one we don't know. That's how the proverb goes. It's clear that the one we don't know must be truly awful."

I scratched my head. "A devil worse than The Devil?"

He nodded. "Much worse, I reckon."

"So who is he, then?"

"That's the point. We don't know him."

"Can't we take a guess?"

He rubbed his chin. "I suppose we could."

"Does he have a name?"

"Probably. But I don't know what it is. That doesn't stop us giving him a nickname. How about Bob?"

I considered this proposal. "Hang about, that's the same as my name! I would prefer to call him something different. What about Dydk? It stands for Devil You Don't Know."

"That's quite neat. Yes, I like it."

"If Dydk is much worse than Satan, then maybe Satan works for him? That would seem logical."

Samuel shook his head. "Satan works for God. It says so in the Bible if you look closely. God uses Satan to test humans by tempting them. Satan is a sort of devil's advocate, so to speak. If God says killing or fornication is bad, then Satan will always put the opposite case. That's his job. I don't believe he would ever moonlight for anyone else, certainly not for a more horrible devil. He's not a traitor."

"In that case, what if God works for Dydk?"

174

"Don't be stupid. God is self-employed. Everyone knows that! Dydk is clearly out of the celestial loop."

"What are you saying?" I demanded.

"Dydk doesn't have anything to do with God or Satan. Perhaps he's not even associated with this cosmos, but comes from another dimension, one adjacent to ours. Who can say? It's not really feasible to make any kind of coherent statement about him at all."

"Because he's the devil we don't know?"

"That's it precisely, Bob!"

I frowned. "Maybe we should stop talking about him? If he's beyond coherence, we're wasting our time."

Samuel smiled. "We can't make a rational statement *about* him, but that doesn't stop us making statements about what he is NOT. Do you follow? Although it's true we can't know him, we can surely know what he isn't. I am permitted to say that he's not a dog, for example. Nor is he an apple or a flute. Nor is he a button or balloon."

"Why can't he be any of those things?" I asked.

"Because we *know* them. And Dydk is the devil we don't know. So his essential attributes must be unknowable."

I had an idea. "If we make a list of ALL the things he isn't, we should get a sort of outline of him. Like an artist who paints the sky all around a tree. Even though he hasn't painted the actual tree, the shape of the tree is there anyway. Let's do this now!"

"You want us to list everything he isn't? But that's everything that can ever be comprehended by the human mind. I don't have several billions of years to spare. Sorry, old friend..."

175

I slapped him on the back. "No panic! The list has already been made for us. It's called the Universe."

And I made a gesture to encompass everything...

But he still wasn't entirely convinced, so I took a scrap of paper and a pencil from my wallet and wrote the words THE UNIVERSE on it and handed it to him. But a sudden gust of wind snatched the paper and took it up into the sky, higher and higher. And we angled our heads upwards to follow its progress. But we found ourselves accidentally staring out of our own universe into an adjacent one.

"Dydk!" Samuel stammered as he fell to his knees.

The thing that now confronted us looked exactly like the blank outline left by listing all knowable things. I fell to my own knees. Then I pointed. I pointed out of the page of this little book up at you. I pointed at you, the reader, sitting there in your chair...

"Dydk!" I screamed at you. Yes, you. You are the devil worse than the devil we know. It was YOU all along!

So now you know.

The Vice-Versa Squad

I am the Two-Toed Sleuth. They call me that in the police department because I like to hang upside-down from trees in my spare time. And because I only have two toes on each foot. I also have two toes on the lobes of both ears, but I don't often talk about those. There's no need.

My real name is Mucky Puppet. I do like to muck around but that's little more than a coincidence. Where my parents come from 'Mucky' is a respectable name. Mind you, they never actually told me where they came from, so maybe I am the victim of a rather cruel deception.

Deception is what we are all about here in the Vice-Versa Squad, perhaps the most elite unit in the entire police force. We do everything backwards. Well, not everything, because we still breathe and eat and talk like normal humans, but when it comes to policing we are obverse.

We commit the crimes before the criminals can.

Needless to say, the criminals get annoyed by this, because we steal all the jewels and leave none for them, rob all the money, kidnap the heirs and heiresses, smuggle the illegal goods through customs, and in short we shoulder them out of the business and into drab unemployment.

In response the criminals organise themselves into groups of detectives and seek us out and arrest us and take us struggling and screaming in improvised vans to the local police station, thus delivering themselves into our hands. How clever and neat is that? We are saved the trouble...

My boss is called Thornton and he always gives me the difficult jobs. I am not sure if this means he likes me or doesn't.

At this moment, for example, I've just entered a gambling den. My mission is to get involved in a poker game and cheat with marked cards. It is dark inside and when I pass through the swing doors I can see hardly anything, just a smoky glow at a point midway along one of the walls.

"What the hell do you want?" demands a harsh voice.

"To get involved in a poker game."

"And you just thought you could walk in here and do that?"

"Of course. Isn't this a gambling den?"

"But you aren't a poker!"

And then someone turns on a table lamp and I see that the room is full of iron rods with sooty ends and other kinds of hearthside appliance and they are all sitting or standing around roulette wheels and dice and dominoes, but there isn't a single playing card anywhere. I have made a mistake, been misinformed, and I turn to leave, but a pair of brass scuttles bar my way and a bellows wheezes at me to remain where I am or there'll be trouble.

But I find it almost impossible to keep my balance with only two toes on each foot, and in fact my normal walk is a sort of controlled lurch, so I stumble and the pokers instantly rush at me and deliver unto me the worst beating of my life, convinced I'm trying to make a dash for it.

I have been a bit floppy ever since and I have dreams. Weird dreams about fire mainly...

The Fire Jump

"Go on, Ashley. We dare you!"

"I don't know if I should. Maybe I'm not strong enough to make the attempt. What if I land in the middle?"

The others laughed. "You're not a coward, are you? What will Cindy say when she finds *that* out?"

"But it's so big!" objected Ashley.

Cole spat his contempt. "If you want to be a member of our fraternity you have to jump it tonight."

"We've all done it," added Burns.

"Go on, Ashley!" cried Smoky. "Make us proud!"

"But I'm simply not ready!"

"Yes you are!" roared Burns, and the others cackled and danced. The moral pressure was so intense that Ashley hesitated for only a few more seconds before suddenly yelling and rushing as fast as he could towards the object of the ritual. As he lifted into the air he realised it was too late to change his mind. The only remaining options were glory or injury. He continued to yell, his throat burning.

It seemed to him that he hung in space for ages, and he was aware of the protruding tongues of his comrades as they watched him soar above the intimidating obstacle. They weren't mocking him now but urging him to succeed. He thought of Cindy and he felt suddenly happy, but when he looked directly down fear gripped him.

The quivering red mass spread in every direction. It was too large and he knew he wouldn't clear it. Then an unexpected gust of wind gave him a slight push that was just enough to propel him to the far side of the ugly throbbing thing. He landed awkwardly but he was safe. Cole, Burns and Smoky began hissing their appreciation.

"I did it! I passed the test! What a laugh!" gasped Ashley.

"You're one of us now," said Cole.

179

"You jumped your first human," declared Burns.

"Congratulations!" added Smoky.

Ashley adjusted his scattered embers. "And a massive human it is too! Obese and sunburnt. I bet he's a tourist. Look at his face! He can't believe what has just happened! He'll be full of stories tonight about the fireball that bounced right over his stomach!"

"Welcome to the club," said Cole. "How do you feel?"

Ashley considered this question.

"Grate!" he said at last.

Taking Time Off

My boss said to me, "Mucky, this department is going down the drain. Too many officers are taking too much time off."

"Because of all the official holidays," I answered.

"That's got nothing to do with it!" he yelled. "I know the couple who are responsible for making official holidays and I'm sure they have the best interests of society at heart. No, I'm talking about *that*!"

And he jabbed with his extended finger at the wall.

On the wall hung a clock without hands or numerals or workings or even a face. In fact it was just a bare patch of wall.

But I couldn't stop looking at my boss's finger and I wondered why it was covered in writing and

180

page numbers. Then I realised it was his index finger, and I congratulated myself on my powers of deduction.

They don't call me the Two-Toed Sleuth for nothing, no sir. They call me it for something, usually a modest sum.

"What do you want me to do?" I asked.

"Find out where they keep taking time off to and fetch it back and prevent them from taking it off again," he told me.

That was a fairly clear set of instructions, so I went away and did what I do best, which is investigating things, and I discovered that the officers were taking time off to a dance hall where an orchestra on a stage played such waltzes as 'The Danube Blues' and 'The Eat Your Greens' and 'The Belly Yellows' and all those old favourites that are nobody's favourite.

It occurred to me that if I could get on the stage I might be able to address the entire gathering and be listened to. Then I could deliver a strong rebuke in my most impassioned voice and shame the officers into taking time back and vowing never to bring it out again. But I wouldn't be allowed on the stage and I forgot to bring my badge, so I had no real authority.

I decided to use my cunning. During the interval I went backstage and gave the conductor a knock on the head when no one was looking. I am as floppy as a blackjack yet hard enough to induce unconsciousness in any average head when I apply myself. I dressed in his attire and during the second half of the show I took his fluorescent baton and his place on stage.

But the musicians began playing immediately and I couldn't be heard over them, so I had to conduct the music and wait for the end of the song, for silence. I had to make it up as I went along, waving my arm with that peculiar electric stick making afterimage patterns in willing retinas.

Someone in the crowd yelled, "Hey, he's supposed to be *keeping* time but he's *beating* it instead! What a bully!"

"Get him!" cried the others; and they did.

They were officers of the law, my former comrades, and they arrested me and charged me with assault, but not with battery, because my fluorescent baton was plugged directly into the mains supply.

A date was arranged for my trial in the high court.

The judge would have given me time. Plenty of it. Luckily it was a holiday and he didn't turn up so I got off lightly.

The Holiday Makers

He used a drill and a hammer, but she preferred a needle and thread. Although they had promised not to race each other, there was rivalry between them. He worked in his shed, but she sat in a rocking chair by the fire. Many hours passed.

The clock struck nine and they put down their tools. He rubbed at the blisters on his palms and she sucked a droplet of blood that the needle had caused to sprout on her thumb.

He entered the house. "Have you finished?"

"Yes." She blinked at him.

"Show me," he said.

"Not before you reveal yours," she replied.

He held up the object he had made and in the firelight it glowed like a coin lost down the side of an inherited sofa so threadbare it has become transparent. She nodded briskly.

"I call it Looking-for-Lost-Things Day," he announced.

"Not bad. What date is it?"

He rubbed his chin with his free hand. "Sometime in late summer or early autumn. How about September 19th?"

She shook her head. "Clashes with Talk-Like-a-Pirate Day."

"That's not one of ours, is it?"

"No, but due to our efforts it became official."

"In that case, I'll make mine September 20th. And yours? Let's see what you've done. Don't be shy."

She revealed her own creation. It resembled a crown for a receptacle that can boil water over a controlled flame. "I call it Wear-a-Tea-Cosy-on-Your-Head Day," she declared.

He was impressed. "What date?"

"August 27th. Nearly fills the gap between Blown-Your-Own-Trumpet Day and the August Bank Holiday."

"Will these new ones catch on, do you think?" he asked.

"Of course. They always do."

"Soon every single day of the year will be a holiday thanks to us. And then the economy will collapse."

"And people will be free from all work…"

He swatted at dark clouds that were forming on his latest masterpiece. "Shame about the weather, though. Wish we could make holidays without generating rain as a by-product."

"Be realistic!" she chided.

The Jungle Bird

It was a big mistake to have an official holiday called Make-an-Apocalypse Day because the citizens of this world took it too seriously and civilisation collapsed in lots of small ways, and all those small ways added up to one big way. And so it was left to me, Mucky Puppet of the Vice-Versa Squad, to get all the survivors organised so humanity could start afresh.

My own view is that there was no point trying, but my boss insisted that I search the remotest jungles on the planet for any isolated communities that might have escaped the disasters. Accordingly I went to Yuckystan and hacked my way through the oppressive and tangled vegetation, but then my cough got better and I found I couldn't go even one step further.

I wondered how others were succeeding or failing at the task, for I was just one of many officers charged with the same mission; and I supposed that a few of the more competent ones were doing better than me. I hung upside-down from an adjacent tree for a few minutes to calm my nerves. Then I heard a voice above me and it said, "Are you having some trouble?"

I turned my head to look and saw a toucan and my face must have betrayed its astonishment because the bird laughed and explained, "There were mutations and I'm a typical result. A talking toucan."

"That's not illegal. You are free to continue," I said.

"But you aren't. This mutated jungle grows at an accelerated rate and it has already sealed itself behind you. Unless I guide you back you will die and there will be nothing left of you but your bones."

"They are floppy," I said, "and might make friends with snakes."

"Is that what you want?"

"No, no, but why should you help me?

"For money, of course! Why else? With my aid you will survive and I will be paid. We must work together."

"I agree with you. If one can't—"

"Toucan," he said; and he guided me through many secret pathways with a remarkable and unerring sense of direction until I was out of the jungle. I found a boat beached on the sands and rowed all the way back to the police station where the Vice-Versa squad had its headquarters.

I asked my boss for cash and presented the toucan to him.

"That's a huge bill," he said.

Loafing Around

They paddled the canoe up the creek to the rotting jetty. In the last rays of the setting sun, they climbed onto the creaking planks and made their way to dry land. The town was silent. No light shone in any window. The rain still dripped from the sagging balconies.

"Looks like we're too late," said Worthington.

185

Nashe shook his head. "We can't be certain of that yet. We'll have to check every single house one by one."

Worthington puffed out his cheeks. "This town has been cut off from civilisation for hundreds of years. Who knows what affect the toxins had on the people who lived here? I mean—"

"That's what we're here to find out. Come on."

But Worthington was wary. "The people of the last town had evolved into giants; and in the town before that, they only had one eye each; and in the town before that... Hideous!"

Nashe shrugged. "You knew the risks."

"Yes, I suppose I did. All the same, it's frightful."

"Let's get it over with, shall we?"

The beam of his heavy torch swinging ponderously in the twilight, his boots squelching dockside mud, he led the way along the waterfront to a row of buildings that turned out to be shops. It was weird seeing them in such a place, in a town surrounded by bubbling green swamps; they were too quaint, pleasant and picturesque.

"Bakers' shops!" breathed Worthington.

Nashe frowned. "All of them, without exception."

Worthington licked his dry lips.

"Look at this display. Braided bread! Seeded rolls and baguettes! And they look fresh. This means that people still live here! The town isn't dead. But where is everyone? Are they hiding?"

Nashe pushed at the front door of every shop. They were all locked for the night with the exception of one at the end of the row. The hinges were oiled and the door swung smoothly open. The two men entered the shop. The torch beams played over shelves packed with bread and cakes. Then Worthington jerked his head and said:

"Shhh! I think I heard something, a rustling…"

Nashe froze, his ears prickling.

He nodded slowly, pointed at one of the largest loaves that stood on a low shelf. The noise was coming from inside it. Worthington joined him and rested his head against the crust.

He hissed, "There are voices within it!"

Nashe reddened, whether from rage or embarrassment was impossible to determine, and he used his free hand to claw apart the loaf. Fistfuls of fluffy bread were scattered in all directions. Worthington retreated a few steps in fear, but his companion was oblivious to danger. He tore with a primal savagery at the whispering loaf.

At last the truth was exposed. A cavern in the heart of the loaf, some sort of cunning refugee for mutants…

The people that were exposed were recognisably human — but none of them were taller than half an inch.

"They have degenerated over many generations!"

"The toxins did this! The toxins!"

"No, I think it was something even worse…"

Nashe was aghast and he rapidly retreated to where Worthington was standing. Both of them crowded the doorway of the shop. They took one last look at the miniature humans; then they ran out into the street, back to the jetty and the safety of the canoe.

"The worse outcome for any isolated community," growled Nashe as he paddled with all his strength to propel them back into the labyrinth of the bubbling swamp, home of snakes with arms and birds with plumage that flashed in colours that hadn't existed before the disaster. It took ten minutes of furious work before they felt secure enough to slow the pace and talk properly again to each other.

"Yes, the worst outcome," agreed Worthington.

"They were tiny! Like imps!"

"Smaller than that. Smaller than my thumb..."

Nashe shuddered and said in an undertone, "I've only ever seen such a situation once before. Down south."

"Horrible. Who could imagine that the entire population... I mean, the entire population... would be..."

"In bread," nodded Nashe with tragic eyes.

Unconvincing Sausage

I'm pleased to say that civilisation didn't waste much time repairing itself and everything soon went back approximately to normal, though there were still plenty of animals roaming around who could speak or who dressed in human clothes. But that was rather nice, I think.

My boss was keen for these animals to be treated equally under the law of the land and he hated it when a pig or elk got off on some technicality related to the fact that the law in question was designed just to cover humans. He thought they were deliberately taking advantage.

So he asked me to disguise myself as a beast and infiltrate their ranks to find out exactly what they were up to. "Listen here, Mucky," he fumed, "because they have sharper senses than we do they think they can outwit us every time, but let's show them they can't! We are men."

"To a greater or lesser extent, yes we are," I said.

"Off you go then!" he urged,

Because I am so floppy I disguised myself as a sausage dog. A very long sausage dog indeed. In this manner I managed to get invited to one of the secret picnics the animals had started having in the deepest part of the woods. Humans weren't allowed, so it was highly risky.

As I made my way along the forest paths I became aware that others were muttering and casting suspicious glances at me. Maybe I just wasn't a competent enough actor. I thought I had perfected the art of acting like a sausage dog but it could be that some minor detail was letting me down, maybe the newspaper that protruded from the pocket of my shorts.

Finally I reached the clearing where the picnic was.

Every place had appropriate cutlery, namely a snake with a forked tongue, a spoonbill for a spoon, a swordfish for a knife, and they had volunteered for the task, which demonstrates how well-organised they really were. After the meal an old elkpig got to its hooves and said—

"Yes, I know I'm a strange hybrid. Blame the radiation. That's not the real point. The real point is that we have finally succeeded in creating a society inside the human society that exactly mirrors it. So we even have a police force and one of the most elite units in that force is called the Vice-Versa Squad and we already have officers disguising themselves as humans and successfully infiltrating every important institution of the human world."

During this speech I was aware that eyes were staring at me. My disguise certainly wasn't good enough, so I did the only thing I could to save my life. I flexed my muscles and burst my costume.

"I'm back!" I cried, standing on my own two feet. "It was difficult getting here without being caught but I managed it. As you can see, I've decided to keep my human costume on just in case I'm needed for another mission. I infiltrated the human Vice-Versa Squad and convinced them I'm working for them. So I'm a double agent. There's a two-toed sloth inside me. Oh curses! the zipper is stuck. You'll just have to take my word for it..."

The Infringement

The door burst open. Three men rushed into the garret like a wedge of frozen spite. The artist in the middle of the room dropped his brush in fright and turned to confront the intruders with wide eyes.

"There he is!" they shouted.

Two of the men were police officers. They stepped forward and seized the artist, dragging him away from his easel.

"W-w-what's going on?"

"You're a thief!" came the contemptuous reply.

"No, I'm not. I've never stolen anything in my life!" protested the artist. "I just paint animals!"

"Exactly! I'm a photographer and I took the photo of that rabbit that you are painting. You're a plagiarist!"

"B-b-but…" stuttered the artist.

"Copyright infringement," said one of the police officers.

"Come quietly," advised the other.

"I was just using the photograph as a guide. There's no harm in that, surely?" objected the artist weakly as he gazed at the unfinished bunny on his canvas.

"A likely story!" The photographer drew a knife and lunged forward, slashing the picture to ribbons.

Later that night, the photographer sat at home, rubbing his hands together with malicious glee. He loved taking legal action against artists who 'borrowed' his images. He was an award-winning wildlife photographer and prints of his best images covered his walls.

Suddenly the door burst open. Three giant rabbits hopped into the lounge and one of them cried, "There he is!"

Two of the rabbits were dressed in police uniforms.

"What's the meaning of this?" blurted the photographer.

"Thief!" growled the first rabbit.

"No, I'm not. I've never stolen anything in my life!" protested the photographer. "In fact I go around prosecuting artists who break the copyright laws."

"Really? But I'm the rabbit that won you an award last month. You stole my image and never paid me for it!" And it nodded at one of the portraits framed on the wall.

"B-b-but…" stammered the photographer.

Before he could get his words out properly, the rabbit policemen bounded forward and gave him a thorough hopping.

The Nose Drill

"Happy birthday," said my boss, because the Earth had travelled round the sun forty times since my birth. "I have a surprise for you. But before you get excited, let me stress it's an unpleasant one."

"That's better than nothing, surely?" I replied.

"Not really, no, it isn't. Listen carefully. The reason you are so floppy isn't because you were beaten by pokers but because you are a puppet. You've always been floppy and always been a puppet."

"Are you serious?" I gasped.

His clown face sagged but the painted smile remained large. "No, but I am telling the truth anyway. You have rubber bones. You don't think I would risk a living person on the hazardous missions I give to you? No, you're a puppet and that explains your surname. Sorry to break the news to you so abruptly but this is a flash fiction. You do understand?"

"There just isn't space or time," I said, nodding.

"Oh there are plenty of both. All together it's known as the universe, but that shouldn't concern you right now. Today your 'Pinocchio' nose came online. It was designed to activate itself on your fortieth birthday. The way it works is very simple. If you tell a lie it grows and if you tell a truth it shrinks again. Why don't you try it out? Try speaking a lie first."

"Statues are living beings," I declared.

To my astonishment, my nose didn't budge. My boss frowned. "Maybe it needs to warm up. Try again in a moment."

I waited and then said, "Coughs live in coffins."

There was a horrid squeaking nose, like hinges so rusty they were beyond any comparison to anything else, and my proboscis jerked out an inch. My boss was so delighted by this that I told another lie. "Tap dancers live in sinks." This time my nose lengthened more smoothly.

"One more!" he chortled. "And then tell three truths."

So I said, "Cats' pyjamas can be exchanged for bees' knees in banks." And then I told three truths, sums like $2+2=4$ and $8x8=64$ and lady(fat)+song=over, and my nose returned to its original length.

I should have stopped there, but some mad impulse made me blurt, "This sentence is untrue!" and all hell broke loose...

I had inadvertently uttered a variant of the notorious Liar's Paradox, which is a sentence that is true and false at the same time but also can't be true and can't be false. In this instance, if my sentence was untrue, as I said it was, it was clearly false, which means it wasn't untrue and thus not false, which means it was untrue after all, which means... and so on forever.

My nose grew and shrank, grew and shrank, grew and shrank, and it did so at such velocity that it was just a blur. It made a shrill whining noise and my boss had to speak up to make himself heard, "Oh dear! But I suppose it can be used as a drill. Not to drill into anything hard like concrete or steel because the drill bit is still the end of a nose, but into a soft substance. Perhaps there is cheese that needs holes somewhere, on an industrial scale?"

The Birth of Opera

The man who thought he knew everything said, "It's not over until the fat lady sings." It was his favourite saying.

"If that's true," came the reply, "how did opera get started?"

"Hey, who said that?"

"I did," answered the statue in the garden.

"Well, I'll be sealed into a barrel and rolled downhill!" exclaimed the man who thought he knew everything.

The statue grinned and winked...

"Statues do come alive every now and then..."

The man who thought he knew everything folded his newspaper and stared at the statue for a long time.

"So you want to know how opera got started in the first place?"

The statue nodded with difficulty. "It wouldn't have been possible if what you said earlier is true. I mean, the moment the fat lady opened her mouth to begin singing, 'it' would be over. That's logic."

And he smirked with an awful creaking noise.

But the man who thought he knew everything brushed some dust from his trousers and said sombrely:

"There's a reason why I'm known as the man who thinks he knows everything and that's because I often do know everything. And I'll answer your question to the best of my ability, which is considerable. Opera got started by the shrieks of the first castrato who was made that way in order to sing higher than any fat lady."

Grammar Police

My boss told me to start arresting people who used grammar incorrectly. It was a mission I dreaded because I wasn't sure what the rules were. After all, I had once taken out a Split Infinitive on a date to an experimental café and had asked her to bravely try one of the wardrobe flavoured ice creams they sold there. She did and announced that it was absolutely pluperfect.

But as I was leaving the station I had a stroke of luck, because at that very moment a man passed me on the pavement and he was mounted on a chariot that was pulled by an aged woman who was the mother of his mother. So I wasted no time chasing him on my tricycle and ordering him to pull over. When he did so, I cried, "That's an incorrect use of a *grammar*."

"You don't understand," he said. "I'm an engineer doing innovative work for the government and this is a prototype."

I arched one of my eyebrows and let it fall flat again with a clank. "Truly? So what precisely is your field of expertise?"

"Nanatechnology," he replied, as he reached into a bag for mints to feed his steed. So I let him go. First person, past tense.

The Reversed Comma

The ordinary comma creates pauses in text; it logically follows that the reversed comma gives prose a push, accelerating it sometimes beyond the point of breathlessness into a blur or scream.

A box of these extremely rare punctuation marks turned up inside a volume on the laws of motion: the pages of that thick tome had been cut away to make a secret hollow space sufficiently large to securely hold the box.

Thornton Excelsior does not remember how the book and thus the box came into his possession. But we know that he once sprinkled a handful of reversed commas into a yellowing copy of the *Highway Code*: the text immediately broke its own laws by exceeding the mandatory speed limit in an urban zone.

Reversed commas are more properly known as *ammocs*, hence the phrase "to run ammoc".

Serious attempts to create interstellar engines by composing entire novels exclusively with reversed commas are destined to fail: nothing can exceed the speed of light entertainment.

Downsizing

The government began insisting that the police force make extensive cuts to its budget. As a consequence the Vice-Versa Squad was told to reduce itself by no less than ninety percent.

My boss was distraught. "They are spending enormous amounts of public money on composing entire novels exclusively with reversed commas, but they can't even give us a million or so to keep us going! Well I am willing to downsize but I won't sack anyone."

And he kept his word.

In fact he actually unlocked the wall safe where his word was stored and he took it to an auction house and sold it. This meant it was impossible for him to ever speak again, but he used the money to pay scientists to shrink the police station and everything inside it.

These scientists were specialists in very small things. They were nanatechnologists and they used ten dozen hefty grannies to sit on the roof and push the walls.

The end result was that the entire police station was reduced in size to little more than one inch in height and width and depth.

The operation was hailed as a great success, but it didn't seem to make me happy. I kept my job but I just never really *fitted in* after this.

I ended up resigning and getting a new job as a bicycle. I don't mean that I wore a bicycle costume but that I had surgery to convert myself into such a machine. Puppets can do that easily.

Brief Hilltop Halt

The cyclist stopped for a drink of water; he also wanted to appreciate the view from the crest of the hill. While his attention was engaged on those twin pursuits, his bicycle wheel struck up a conversation with a bent tree that grew close to the rough track.

"Your fruit doesn't look ripe," the bicycle said.

"Fruit? The month is April; there aren't any fruits on trees at this time of year. I'm just about to blossom."

The tree spoke by rustling its leaves; the result was a sibilant hiss that made everything seem like a secret.

The bicycle considered the answer it had been given and said, "If that's so, what's this object hanging here?"

"It's a bud," hissed the tree.

"Buddhist?" The bicycle was bewildered.

"I didn't say it was a Buddhist, I said it was a bud," hissed the tree in mild annoyance. The bicycle intoned:

"You didn't say it was a Buddhist, you said it was a Buddhist?"

"A bud, not a Buddhist!"

"I distinctly heard the sound *bud hissed…*"

"That's impossible. I didn't say the word 'hissed', I only said the word 'bud'. The word 'hissed' was outside the speech marks. It doesn't refer to what I said but to the way I said it."

The bicycle digested this information slowly.

"What religion is it then?"

"What religion is what?" The tree was exasperated.

"The bud," clarified the bicycle.

"Oh that, I think it's a Zoroastrian," said the tree.

The Bicycle Mine

I didn't last long as a bike. Who does? I hate being saddled with responsibilities and the weight of all those cyclists on my frame all day was too much to bear, so I quit and became unemployed. Unable to pay the mortgage I lost my house and was made homeless. It was at this point that I asked myself aloud a question that subconsciously had bothered me for a long time, "Where do all the real bicycles come from?" Because the fact is that I didn't know. I knew for certain that people could be turned into bicycles, but those weren't the *original* kind. No, I hoped to locate the source of the very first bicycles.

I had no restrictions anymore, I could come and go as I liked and so didn't need to worry about anything but pleasing myself. I set off with my possessions wrapped in a spotted handkerchief and tied to the end of a pole that I carried over one shoulder. I don't actually know what possessions were in there but they were *meagre*; I had been told that a penniless wanderer is supposed to have that kind. I like to do things properly. I tramped out of the city and through a forest and over a range of mountains and across a desert and through a marsh and finally came to a region where the ground had been opened.

I mean that it was a place full of mines and quarries and the way that nature had been spoiled was dreadful. I saw that there were mines for a great

199

variety of commercial products that the urban dweller takes for granted. For example, here was a hole where clothes, including hats and gloves, were chiselled from the bowels of the earth and brought up into the light. And another mine was the source of all the coffee that is drunk in fashionable cafés, huge nodules of the stuff being winched up from narrow shafts and bashed into beans by hammers on the surface. And then I saw the bicycle mine.

"Hey you!" cried the manager. "You have a drill for a nose and so I reckon you should start working here immediately."

"It's a wooden nose, the nose of a puppet, and will break if used against a substance as hard as rock. So I must refuse."

"I won't take no for an answer. If you can't do any drilling to excavate the bicycles, then operate this pump instead."

I was seized by his henchman and dragged over. But I didn't know what I was supposed to be doing and I worked the pump too hard and overinflated the ores in which the tyres were embedded, far beneath, and there was an explosion and raw bicycles and dead workers were flung everywhere. Every time a piece of rubble rushed towards me, my vibrating nose annihilated it before it could smash my face. It hurt the tip something rotten though! In fact my nose was bent totally and absurdly out of shape. Twisted back on itself, it was almost embedded in my chin, giving my face a handle. Dust settled.

I found a bicycle that wasn't badly damaged and made my escape, but I got rid of it soon after by trading it for a potato.

Potato Soup

Three penniless wanderers met on a lonely road and said, "Let's camp here for the night and keep each other company." So they lit a fire on the verge from sticks and logs and huddled around it. One of them had a cooking pot and he set some water to boil, but when it was bubbling furiously they discovered they had nothing to put into it.

"A fine meal this will be!" sighed the first wanderer.

"Just hot water!" sniffed the second.

"Wait a moment!" cried the third as he felt in his bag. "I think I've found an old potato. Let's boil that and have potato soup!"

They were excited by this development and happy to watch the potato rise and fall in the pot. After twenty minutes of being boiled they each took a spoon and sampled the soup.

The first wanderer said, "I can taste buttons!"

The second said, "It tastes of pockets."

And the third made a face and grumbled, "It tastes to me like a collar. I wonder what this means?"

They pondered for a long time.

Then the first wanderer said, "My confidence was coming apart but the buttons of this soup are holding it together again and I feel much more positive about the future…"

The second wanderer said, "I had nowhere to put my dreams before eating this meal, but now I can keep them in the pockets that I've just digested and I won't worry so much about losing them…"

The third wanderer said, "The collar of this repast will enable me to keep warm whenever I reach

201

the *neck* of the woods. This is good news for all of us, but how did it happen?"

The other two wanderers shrugged.

Suddenly the third wanderer clapped his hands. "I know why. It's obvious now. It was a jacket potato!"

Heavens Ajar

Eventually I managed to find a new job, but it was dangerous work, and when I complained to my employer he snarled and said, "You don't really have a choice, do you? There are thousands of other people working in much more hazardous jobs than you are. Count yourself lucky."

I frowned at him. There was something familiar about his features. "Do I know you from somewhere?" I inquired.

"Don't be silly, Mucky. We've never met before. I don't even know your name! You don't really think I'm your former boss at the Vice-Versa Squad who is now in disgrace and was forced to disguise himself and work here? The same guy who sold his word and can't speak?"

"I apologise. Don't fire me."

"Just take your ladder and get to work!"

My new job, I must explain, was to jam wide the heavens when they next opened and keep them open so that people could enter them without needing to die first. That was the big idea anyway.

And did the heavens open often? Yes, if the weather reports were to be believed. "The heavens opened today!" And so it was essential that I rush to the scene of the opening, prop my ladder against the best available cloud and climb the rungs.

And when I got high enough I would thrust a wooden wedge into the gap to ensure the heavens couldn't close again.

But I was always too late. Not once did I ever see an actual hole leading from our world into heaven, and so I began wondering if the job had been invented just to get me off the streets. If so, should I be grateful or resentful? I didn't know.

Then one day people started screaming in the city streets and I went to investigate.

"Oh God!" they shouted.

A cloud shaped like an edible fungus was rising into the sky and I recalled how tasty fungi are when cooked with potatoes, but there seemed to be a figure inside the cloud.

If people had seen God it logically followed that at long last the heavens had opened at the right time for me, so I propped my ladder against the cloud and started climbing and then I have no idea what happened.

I woke up in a room with metallic walls and faces were peering at me through portholes and a loudspeaker by my head crackled into life.

"You got a nasty dose of radiation," said my boss.

"Is it fatal?" I whimpered.

"Not for a puppet, but it hasn't made you any prettier."

"Poor me!" I sighed.

"Look on the bright side, Mucky."

"Why should I do that?"

"You have no choice, you glow in the dark."

203

The Mushroom Cloud

The mushroom cloud rose high over the desert. The men who watched it weren't sure what kind of mushroom it might be.

One of them flicked through a book on the identification of fungi but he didn't find anything on any page resembling the tower of smoke that was growing on the horizon. Nonetheless it was a mushroom cloud. Everyone knew this.

"Why does nobody ever call them toadstool clouds?" someone said.

"Shut up!" growled another.

"But no, really, it would make more sense..."

"Shut up, I said! It wouldn't make more sense at all, just an equal amount of sense. An equal amount isn't more!"

"I guess you're right. Sorry."

"We've got no time for these stupid conversations. Listen here, Upton, I want you and Schulz to go out there and see if you find some of that special glass that's always made after one of these tests."

"Special glass? You mean *trinitite*, which is light green in colour and a typical product of nuclear explosions in deserts?"

"That's the kind, sure enough."

"And what do we do if we find any?"

"Bring as much back as you can carry. Take a jeep and load it up."

"But is it safe out there?"

"You'll be wearing radiation suits, naturally.

"Will they be adequate?"

"I don't know. Just do it. That's an order! You can keep half the glass you collect as payment."

"What use will that be to us?"

"You can sell the goddamn stuff. Now get moving!"

Upton had no choice but to obey. He and Schulz went off to fetch a couple of suits from the storerooms. In the distance the mushroom cloud was still expanding. The reason why it wasn't a toadstool cloud, Upton suddenly realised, was because there wasn't a giant fairy sitting on the top of it.

The Archdruid raised the oak branch that was his wand and intoned words of ancient and lyrical gibberish over the altar stone. It was the summer solstice, the most important night in the calendar for him and his pagan brethren. The circle of standing stones stood around them and gleamed in the firelight.

Suddenly two strange figures approached him. They came out of the night, out of the shadows, and they were like twisted forest spirits, hideously scarred and wearing dark glasses despite the fact the sun had already gone down.

Before the Archdruid could protest at this intrusion, one of the figures forced a smile onto his horrid face, gestured at the standing stones around them, specifically at the gaps between the uprights and the lintels that capped them, and said:

"Bit draughty in here, isn't it? Can we interest you in some double glazing?"

Whirlpool Face

I finally had enough money to pay for an expensive operation on my nose. It was broken and needed to be straightened, but I also wanted it to stop oscillating and making that annoying buzzing noise that continually distracted me. Like so many other entities, I wanted a stable normal nose.

The private clinic that accepted me made a big fuss about the difficulties of the procedure, but that was just talk to ease their consciences about the amount of money they were charging, which was half my compensation from the ladder job. The sum was handed over and I got a receipt.

Then a mechanic appeared and straightened my nose with a spanner.

There was no anaesthetic. "Ouch! Did I pay just for *that*?" But no, they assured me that the main operation was the one to stop the oscillating. The straightening was just a spanner in the works. But I think they had got their sayings mixed up.

Anyway I was wheeled on a trolley into the theatre. The actors and audience were plainly annoyed at being hustled out to make space for me. They had been enjoying a performance of *King Lear*. The surgeon came over with a starched smile and aimed it at me, and I felt like a cockroach in a flashlight beam, ready to scuttle under the breadbin.

"I'm a puppet and so need something strong to put me under," I said.

"Punch," replied the surgeon.

"Don't hit me!" I pleaded. "I can feel pain!"

"Which is why we are giving you the anaesthetic! But when I said 'punch' I meant an alcoholic drink. Rum and fruit."

They brought in a bowl of this and I drank it down. I recall thinking that it was odd that the bowl had a sort of spiral pattern engraved on the inside, like one of those maelstroms they have out at sea. But I said nothing, I just glugged it into my puppet tummy, that potent concoction.

And yes it knocked me out. And the next thing I knew... well, I was lying on a soft bed blinking my wooden eyelids.

"When does the operation start?" I asked a nurse.

"It's over," she replied. "Your nose won't ever oscillate again. We couldn't get at the paradox directly, so we did some surgery on your brain and cut out the parts that enable you to lie. It's now impossible for you to ever tell an untruth. A nose with a 'Pinocchio' setting like yours can't grow at all unless you tell lies, so the oscillating has ceased. Clever, huh?"

"Ingenious," I said. But I was apprehensive.

Now I can only speak the truth and so my nose will shrink until it is flush with my face, but can I be sure it will stop there?

What if it starts boring into my head, a backfiring nose, a Pinocchio proboscis in reverse? Will it create a crater in my visage, a whirlpool that might suck in all objects in the vicinity?

Might the former Two-Toed Sleuth become a maelstrom of his own or even a black hole?

I vowed never to speak another word in my lifetime, so I wept instead.

The nurse was unsympathetic.

"Come now. Cease blubbing. Others have had much worse experiences in the operating theatre than you have!"

Black Ops

When he reached the reception desk, Thornton Excelsior said, "I've come about the vacancy advertised in the newspaper. I have experience in all the necessary areas and I—"

The receptionist pointed at a door. "Go through there. Dr Vaughan and Dr Frazer require you immediately."

Thornton paused. "Don't I get an interview? Don't I even need to fill out an application form for the job?"

The receptionist shook her head emphatically. This struck him as odd, but he reminded himself that the position was in *Black Ops*, so irregular procedures were probably normal. Perhaps they were testing him in some obscure fashion? He went through the door and found himself in gloom. A voice from nowhere said, "Are you new?"

Thornton stuttered, "Yes, I saw the advert in the paper and—"

"You start at once! Get ready!"

Another voice, equally bodiless snapped, "Scalpel!"

Thornton dared not move a muscle.

The first voice cried, "What are you waiting for? Pass him the scalpel! Hurry man, we don't have all day!"

Thornton lurched forward and tripped over something. He got slowly to his feet, steadying himself by resting his hands on a low table just in front of him. Something soft and wet lay there. His fingers felt sticky now. He groped around with them and felt a sharp pain along the back of his hand. The second voice barked in his ear:

"What are you doing? You're not operating on yourself!"

"Clamps!" screamed the first voice.

"Tie off that vein there, you oaf!" growled the first.

Thornton retreated, knocked the back of his head on a machine that started emitting a series of frantic beeps. He gasped, "I have experience in the relevant areas! I know all about sabotage, propaganda, disorientation! I can manipulate foreign media—"

The owner of the first invisible voice made no attempt to conceal his contempt. "This is a circumcision!"

"But in the dark—" objected Thornton.

The second voice snarled, "Black Ops, you fool! Get out! Get out and don't ever return! Time waster!"

After he had finally managed to fumble his way out of the unseen door back into the world of light and visible shapes, a weak third voice floated up from the vicinity of the table.

"Another bloody spy!" it croaked.

The Nosedive

I am no longer Mucky Puppet. I can never be mucky again, nor a puppet. I can't ever be anything at all in any way. I remained silent, but silence is often the truest truth. If anyone said something that was true in my vicinity, my lack of response was taken as an agreement, a reinforcement of the truth that had been uttered, and thus it constituted a truth itself. So my nose retracted into my face and kept going and made a hole that became a black hole.

Everything near me was sucked into my head and compressed into a dot as big as nothing, a singularity, even objects larger than I am, such as tables, cellos and mountains. My boss is within, and so are the bicycle mines, gambling dens, jungles, clocks, canoes and opera houses. I am devouring the planet and it won't be long before I get to you too. Worst of all, common sense has been sucked into me and there's none left. Only rare sense.

F I N I S

As you managed to get this far in one piece, here's a bonus microfiction for you. It's only twelve words long:

I once knew a papaya that was buried in a pawpaw's grave.

It doesn't have a title but I guess I could call it 'Fruity Funeral' if I had to...

Thanks for reading!

Rhys Hughes was born in 1966 and has published 29 books and written more than 720 short stories in the past two decades and his work has been translated into ten languages. When not writing, he spends his time mountaineering, dabbling with music and lazing around indoors and outdoors. To find out more please visit: http://rhyshughes.blogspot.com

Brankica Bozinovska is an illustrator and air traffic controller from Macedonia. A beautiful, stylish and multi-lingual lady in real life she is also a bold and wise fictional character in Hughes' as-yet unpublished novel *The Pilgrim's Regress*. Her drawings are difficult to obtain and aren't currently for sale at the moment.

It seems to me you deserve another microfiction.

Why not? They aren't especially fattening or bad for your health in any other way. This one is called 'Saucy Jean'...

When he climbed the staircase in his bare feet, I could hear him coming.

That's how I knew his name was Cocteau.

Now it really is time to say bye bye!

Bye bye!